I have developed a detachment f̣
I don't fear them. I don't considɛ
that I genuinely loathe them. The
abused as a child. There were no
adolescence, no heartbreak or reȷ ...... *childhood.*
Nothing to account for the person I have become. I shall offer
no explanation, no mitigation for what I am. But whatever the
reason, I have come adrift from mankind, and that is where I
intend to stay.

Welcome to Gary Lennon's world. It isn't a cold dead place.
You'll like it there. You'll see things his way and you'll want to
stay. But Gary's therapist has other ideas. He thinks Gary
should get a job, meet people and interact with the real world.
Look out, people. Look out, world.

"Gary is an anti-hero for our times, Everyman and the Outsider
rolled into one, and his zeitgeist will explode off the page and
roll down your chin with each mounting episode."
John Lake (author, *Hot Knife*)

The World is (Not) a Cold Dead Place

Nathan O'Hagan

Published by Armley Press 2015

Cover Design: Mick Lake & Nathan O'Hagan

Layout: Ian Dobson

Contact: <info@armleypress.com>

ISBN 0-9554699-9-6

"For Emily. For everything."

Thanks to Mick McCann, John Lake, Mick Lake, Andy O'Hagan, Elaine O'Hagan, Julie Shaw, Rob Heath, Judith Williamson and Steve Rycroft.

ONE

"Fucking smackheads and perverts, that's the kind of people Birkenhead is full of. 'The one-eyed town' they call it. It's like Mecca for these scum. They migrate here. I don't know what it is about this fucking town, but it just draws them in. Or they're just moved here by social services or whatever. You know why that is, don't you?"

I shake my head slightly, without making eye contact. The strange man takes a step closer to me, leaning his head conspiratorially close to mine.

"It's the big old Victorian houses. They're cheap round here you see. Try buying that kind of house down south or even in the midlands. It'll set you back close to half a million, whereas round here you can get one for less than two hundred thousand. Bit of a difference isn't it? And houses like that, they're easily converted. Knock down a few walls, convert the odd basement, and you can house at least five or six of these people in the one place. Buy two properties next door to each other, knock them through into one; there's room enough for about twelve paedo's, smack heads, rapists or whatever scum bag you like."

I notice a few commuters turn their heads slightly to look at me. Anyone can see what is happening here, that I am desperate for help. But, of course, nobody intervenes. This is modern Britain. Nobody is about to stick their neck out for you.

"'Halfway Houses' they used to call them. Or 'Rehabilitative Units' these days. As if people like that can be rehabilitated. Meanwhile, the Catholic church in the North End has been boarded up for years. Fixing it up is clearly not very high on the Vatican's to-do list. I wouldn't be surprised if they end up shoving a load of deviants in there too. Fucking hell, if Jesus ever did come back to see that, we'd have a whole new 'angry-Jesus-in-the-temple' story wouldn't we?"

I have no idea who this man is. I have never laid eyes on him before, and I certainly did not instigate any discussion with him. But some people apparently need no invitation. Some people think they have the right to talk to anyone they choose. Just because I happen to be standing in the same train station as him, he has taken that as licence to start up a conversation. Although conversation is probably not the right word. 'Conversation' implies two people talking to each other, rather than one individual talking *at* an unwilling second participant.

But standing in Birkenhead's Hamilton Square station, with its windy, black tunnels representing the only possibility of escape, I am pretty much a captive audience. I still don't know why he chose me out of the many people down here. I doubt I look approachable, so maybe he has already done the rounds of everyone else on the platform at some time or other, and it is simply my turn. I don't possess the skills necessary to extricate myself from this predicament so, instead, I begin to edge my way along the platform away from this man. He doesn't take the hint though, and simply follows me along the yellow safety line, still continuing his diatribe.

"Did you know Wallasey has the second highest recorded rate of incest in the known world? There's some tiny village in deepest darkest Peru, where they do it as the norm, that has the highest. Then Wallasey. Can you believe that? Something to do with all the kids from single parent families, who have no idea who their father is, unwittingly sleeping with half sisters and half brothers and cousins. Jesus. Involuntary incest. My brother used to be a social worker you see, so I know the figures, and believe me mate, it's bloody scary. We've got the highest concentration of paedophiles per square mile in the U.K. Same with the druggies. There are so many of them that, statistically, there are probably about ten paedos in this station alone."

I wonder what he is basing this statistical analysis on, but I don't want to give him any encouragement, so I keep my mouth shut.

"It's getting worse too, because of all the flats they built around here during the property boom. Since the arse fell out of the market, they can't get rid of them. So instead of having block upon block of flats standing empty, the council puts pressure on the people who own them to sell them off to these private charities and hospitals which look after people like that. But which is worse? Empty flats or flats full of sex offenders and drug addicts? I know which one I'd rather have. And no council wants its borough overrun by deviants, so there must be something else in it for them. Somewhere, someone's palm is getting greased. It always is. Someone is benefiting financially

8

from letting these bastards roam our streets."

The more I edge away, the more he follows me, his voice getting a bit louder, his manner more agitated, and a slightly deranged look developing in his eyes. The scary thing is, this is not some raving derelict. This man is middle aged, wearing a suit and carrying a briefcase and umbrella. He, like the majority of the people here, is on his way to work. He isn't one of those mentally unstable homeless people who ride the train all day long, only disembarking occasionally so they can swear at strangers on the platform. He isn't about to stab me in the eye or set me on fire. But to me, unwanted social interaction is its own very specific brand of violence. The stranger walks right up to me and leans in even closer.

"You always have to look for who stands to benefit in these situations. Now, if you ask me – "

"But I didn't ask you did I?" I whisper back to him. I would be more than entitled to shout, but I am not prepared to draw unwanted attention to myself by raising my voice.

"You fucking what?"

"I said I didn't ask you. I didn't want this. I'm just waiting for a train. It was you that started talking to me, without invitation I might add. Do you even realise that you have just pursued me along half the length of this platform, just so you can carry on this rant? Are you aware of how insane that makes you look? You were in such a frenzy you didn't even realise that I was trying to escape you. I don't need anyone to tell me how bad this town is; I live in it."

"Who the hell do think you're – " the man attempts to interrupt me, but I just talk over him.

"I see the same scum bags drinking cans of lager on street corners first thing in the morning. I see the same women walking to the shops in their fucking pyjamas and slippers. I have the same smack heads blocking my path to ask me to spare them some change. Those gangs of teenagers driving around in their ridiculously fitted out cars, with their banging fucking techno blasting out of the window? I see them too. You're not the only person it affects. The last thing I need is for a stranger to tell me just how decrepit Birkenhead is. I already know. And as for the stuff about the church in the North End; yes, I understand what you're trying to say; God has forsaken Birkenhead. And who can

9

fucking blame him? I don't need that spelling out for me. So please, for fuck's sake, just leave me alone. Seriously, just walk away from me. Go and harangue someone else if you must, but please, *please* just leave me alone."

The man looks almost dazed, as though I have just clicked my fingers to bring him out of some sort of trance. He looks down at the platform, seemingly having forgotten where he is.

"I...I'm sorry," he mutters, a look of shame crossing his face. I accept the man's apology, and he finally walks away, back to the end of the platform where his pursuit of me first began. I accept his apology because I know it's not really his fault. That slightly maniacal look I saw in his eyes, I see it in the eyes of just about everyone on the platform, every time I come here. The train pulls in to the station and, as I board it, I watch the expressions on the faces of the hundreds of people change. I feel the angst increase around me as their time draws nigh.

I stand near the door, ignoring the few filthy-looking empty seats in the cramped carriage. I watch as people read books and newspapers, nervously fiddle with their iPods or mobiles, or just stare blankly ahead, silently praying for the train to crash, for terrorists to attack, or for the walls of the tunnel to collapse, flooding us with the filthy, polluted water of the River Mersey. Anything to stop them having to go into work. That's why I can just about excuse the stranger's behaviour, because only yesterday it was Sunday, and these people were all free and enjoying their weekends. And then, as the evening approached, they will all have begun to get that feeling in their stomachs. That same feeling that I used to get on a Sunday evening when I was a kid, knowing that I had to go back to school in the morning. That horrible, knotted feeling of nervous tension. They will have been feeling that since last night, but so much worse. Some of them will have felt it so bad, it would have caused them to double over in agony, and now it will be increasing by the second, and will continue to do so until they get to their places of work. So I recognise and understand their tension, but I don't share it, because I am not going to work. These people are living the nightmare, I'm just visiting.

As they all stand to leave the train at James Street, Moorfields and Lime Street, I simply decide not to complete my journey, and continue on the loop back to Hamilton Square. I have no job to go to. In fact, at the age of twenty eight, I can honestly say I have never done what could reasonably be described as a hard day's work in my life.

I am unemployed, having been deemed unfit for work due to varying levels of Obsessive Compulsive Disorder, Social Anxiety Disorder, agoraphobia, depression, paranoia and the frequent occurrence of panic attacks. I have, over the years, also developed a growing detachment from the rest of the human race. I don't fear them. I don't even consider myself above them necessarily. It's just that, for the most part, I genuinely loathe them.

There is no reason for the way I am. I wasn't abused, or even neglected as a child. I was never subjected to bullying through my school years. There were no traumatic events during my puberty or adolescence. I experienced no heartbreak or painful rejection during early adulthood. Nothing that could account for the kind of person I have become. I shall offer no explanation, no mitigation for what I am. But whatever the reason, I have come adrift from mankind. I exist only on the periphery of society, and that is where I intend to stay.

So, as much as I hate having to occasionally descend into the hell of public transportation in this way, it does have its advantages. It's a reminder of how my life might have been if I had made different choices, and validation of the choices that I have made. Everyone else is here because they have to be, but I can leave at any moment. The life I lead may be desolate by most standards, but at least I don't have to endure this particular misery every morning.

TWO

"Do you masturbate?"

For the last two and a half years, I have been forced to see a psychiatrist. The dole send me here, as they will do on rare occasions with hopeless cases like me who've been in receipt of benefits for a long time, to make sure I'm not faking it, and no doubt to see if they can find a reason to cut off my money. I visit him at the same time every week: Thursday, 11 o'clock. My therapist is a middle aged, overweight man called Brian and every week I come here, sit in his office, with its self-consciously modern décor, and for an hour he sits opposite me, the buttons of his shirt straining to contain his fat gut, and asks me questions about myself, which I try to answer as frankly and as honestly as I can. He then reports back to the dole that I'm still unable to work, and I know that my next fortnightly money is safe. There is a stigma attached to this kind of therapy and, having had to endure it for so long, I can fully understand why. It's like being given a full body cavity search. I find Brian's analysis simplistic and unoriginal, and most of the time, I leave with the feeling that I need another shower.

For the last couple of weeks Brian has been a little bit pre-occupied with my sexuality. Or my complete lack thereof. It has now been several years since I last had sex. This is not because I am unattractive; I think most women would tell you that I'm quite good looking. Nor is it because I don't like sex; I certainly understand the brief feeling of physical pleasure that sexual release can bring to people. The real reason is that I have come to find it almost unbearable to be touched by other human beings. I have always had intimacy issues, but these have gradually worsened over time so that the gap between each sexual assignation and the next grew larger and larger, until I reached the point where I found myself struggling to bear any kind of physical contact. This includes a hug. I even find handshakes uncomfortable, and have on occasion begun carrying around small packets of hand-wipes so I can clean my hands if I find myself in a situation where a handshake is unavoidable. These days, the closest I get to sexual release is a good solid bowel movement.

12

While he awaits my response, Brian fiddles with the blue cord around his neck, from which hangs one of those photo-id cards mental health professionals wear, before placing it back between the pair of man-breasts he has grown over the last couple of years. This is the kind of intrusive and deeply personal question Brian can throw in at any time. I would quite like to tell him it's none of his business, spit in his chubby red face and walk out. But if I did that, my money would probably stop, giving Brian a certain power over me which I deeply resent, and I'm sure that sometimes he throws in this kind of question just to exercise that power.

"Sometimes."

"How often?"

"Not as much as I used to, maybe once or twice a week, if that."

"Are you still using pornography?"

"Using? That's a fairly stupid choice of word. If you mean do I still *watch* porn, then yes, but nowhere near as much as I used to, and even when I do, I often just watch it. Sometimes I'll watch it but not actually masturbate to it."

"And why do you think this is Gary?"

"Well, seeing as you're the professional, why don't you tell me why you think this is, instead of trying to make me do your job for you?"

"Fair enough. I think that you still watch porn because, however deeply you've tried to bury them, you still have sexual needs and urges. I think you curb your urge to masturbate as often as you used to because you fear that, the more you masturbate, the more you will feel the need for actual sex and the more you feel this need, the more likely it is that you will have to actually attempt to meet a girl and begin a sexual relationship, and you've made it very clear that a sexual relationship, or indeed any kind of relationship, is not something you are currently interested in, which is really very unfortunate, as I think that meeting a girl might actually be very good for you."

I slowly raise my hands up in front of my face, before applauding sarcastically.

"That's the kind of predictable assessment I've come to expect from you Brian; imitative, devoid of insight or originality," I say, "as for the meeting a girl part, that's really not

13

likely to happen Brian."

"I understand you find this extremely difficult, but I'm very concerned about this matter. The longer you continue without intimacy and without physical contact, the more you'll make it into an insurmountable obstacle, and if you continue much longer I fear you may render yourself incapable of forming any sort of relationship in the future, and this worries me."

"It's not just a case of finding this 'extremely difficult' Brian. You say 'meeting a girl' as though it's something perfectly simple and natural, but to me it's impossible. I can't participate in those mating rituals that other people engage in so easily. I'm not one of those strutting peacocks who can see a girl, home in on her and approach her without hesitation. For fuck's sake Brian, I'm sitting here talking to you because I can barely leave my flat without having a panic attack, so what makes you think I would ever be capable of something like that? And besides, it's not just a case of being incapable. I have neither the ability nor the inclination to pursue such things. You see, it's not just the whole sex and intimacy thing. It's the whole social networking thing too."

Brian looks confused.

"What do you mean by the whole social networking thing?" he asks.

"Well, what I mean is that for every new person you meet, the chances are that you will at some point have to meet dozens of other people associated with them. For example, if I meet a girl I will almost certainly have to meet her friends, then her friends' boyfriends, then their friends, and on and on it goes. And even if her friends are mostly tolerable people, there will usually be an over-protective best friend who will, at the earliest available opportunity, drag me into a corner and subject me to a prolonged drunken rant about how lucky I am to be seeing her best friend, how special she is and how I had better not ever dare hurt her. And should I overcome these initial hurdles and get into something approaching a relationship with a girl, there is the probability that I will then have to meet her family, which involves all kind of socially awkward interactions during which I have to pretend to be interested in what her parents do for a living, what college course her younger brother is on or what fucking tricks the family dog has recently learned. And this is

14

just the beginning. This is before you even get to the extended family, with their weird cousins, senile grandparents and lecherous uncles. I mean, why the fuck would I want to subject myself to this kind of thing? Why would *anyone* want to subject themselves to that kind of thing? And if you survive all that shit, then somewhere down the line, most women are likely to start talking about kids."

"And is that really such a bad thing?"

"You got kids Brian?"

"This is probably not something I should be discussing, but as a mater of fact I have two kids. A boy and a girl."

"And do you enjoy lying to them?"

"Why would I lie to my kids Gary?"

"When they come to you and ask about what life is really all about. When they ask you why we're here, why we struggle through our existences, whether it is all worth it. Whether there really is any hope for mankind, and whether you're glad that you brought them into this twisted world, if you're happy that you have doomed them to a lifetime of pointless drudgery. Do you enjoy having to tell them that there is a point to it all, that the world is full of hope and beauty? How does it make you feel to have to lie to them like that, and to know that by bringing any child into this world, you have in fact committed a gross act of cruelty? And doesn't it fill you with horror to realise you can't protect them from the evil this world is full of? To know that you are powerless to insulate them from the hideous things that human beings do to each other constantly? Doesn't it make you feel truly impotent?"

I wait for Brian to respond. He exhales deeply, looks down at the floor and shakes his head slightly. He takes a deep breath, then he looks up at the clock on his wall.

"Time's up", he says.

That night, I am gripped by a certain curiosity. What Brian and I talked about earlier has been playing on my mind. I get up from the couch and walk to my bedroom wardrobe. In a bedraggled old cardboard box at the bottom of it is my porn collection. In this box is a detailed cross-section of the entire "adult entertainment" industry. Every aspect of the industry is represented, from glossy, elaborately plotted studio productions starring beautiful women with bouffant hair and perfect skin, to low budget "gonzo" films featuring dead-eyed women engaging in progressively more degrading sex acts with men whose faces rarely appear on camera. I root through the videos, DVDs and magazines and choose something from the middle of the pornographic spectrum, *Extreme Gang Bangs Volume 3*, and take it back into the living room. I put the video in the machine, sit back on my couch, and hit the play button. Instantly the TV screen is filled with a mass of naked bodies. I stare at the screen as the deluge of human flesh writhes and contorts, each body part seemingly indistinguishable from the next. Until recently this kind of film provided me with my only sexual outlet. If I felt the need, I could put one of these videos on and find a simple form of release. Now though, the bodies don't seem like bodies, they seem like some hideous breed of snake, all intertwining, trying to strangle the life from each other. The noises coming from the TV seem strange and inhuman. Far from being sexy, the whole thing is a little unsettling. I think about bulimic teenage girls, with plastic bags full of vomit hidden under their beds, and wonder if my porn stash is any less pathetic. I put my hand on my cock to see if it has responded in any way. Nothing. I take the tape out of the machine and snap it in half, and hurl the two parts against the wall.

I run back to my bedroom wardrobe and take my box of porn and tip the contents into a bin bag, which I take downstairs and stuff into a wheelie bin. I then place a bag of normal rubbish on top of it and force it deep down. I punch the top bag as hard as I can, grazing my knuckles against the bottles and cans inside, pushing the pornography as far down into the bin as it can possibly go, burying it amongst the crap and garbage. I spit into the bin and slam the lid shut on the last vestiges of my libido.

THREE

Beep beep beep beep beep beep beep beep beep beep beep beep beep beep... Unbelievable. Every weekday morning, Monday to Friday at exactly the same time; 8.40am. For the last three weeks I've been awoken by the sound of a car alarm going off outside the house opposite my flat. It has been driving me mad, and, from the snippets of conversation I've overheard, I know it's been the cause of much consternation amongst my neighbours. It's clear that the constant chirping of that shrill car alarm is becoming a nuisance. Of course, car alarms by their very existence *are* a nuisance, but there will always be money to be made by providing a gullible public with the illusion of security, so the car alarm industry continues to thrive.

In the conversations I've overheard there are a couple of recurring questions: "Why that same car?" and "Why always at the same time?" I believe I know the answers to both these questions. Firstly, the car in question is a brand new metallic grey Mercedes. A Mercedes which, in a significant step up, replaced the owner's previous car, a Ford Focus. According to some of the conversations I have overheard, the man in question was only able to buy it because a few months ago a wealthy aunty died, bequeathing him a significant amount of money in her will, which he decided to spend in one go on this vehicle. The houses on my street are pretty evenly split between family homes with appropriate cars parked outside, and buildings that have been converted into flats and bedsits, most of which are populated by people like me, who either don't drive or can't afford a car.

Before this one arrived, the only time I had seen a Mercedes on the street was when the local fire crew had to extinguish one that had been set alight and abandoned by joyriders a couple of doors down from my flat.

The reason why this car has been targeted is, I believe, quite simple. It's not through jealousy, or even a wanton and destructive urge to vandalise, but because the children passing through my street on their way to school see this beautiful car parked in this modest street and, in their own primitive way, understand that this man has ideas above his station. He's saying he's better than the rest of us, or at least different somehow. The children, always quicker than adults to stamp ruthlessly on any signs of individuality, understand this, and in their own inarticulate way are letting him know that they understand. The throwing of the stone is their way of taking him down a peg or two. I know exactly why they're doing it, and I also know that I will never be targeted in such a way. To people like them I am invisible, as I will never aspire to the ownership of any such status symbol. But then, I never really aspired to anything much.

So once again my sleep is broken by that alarm. I know I have no chance of getting back to sleep now, so I walk down the road to the mini market so I can buy a packet of ciggies and a pint of milk.

Shops are strange places, always brimming with people just dying to make a connection with someone. I wonder how many people in any shop at any given time actually need to buy anything, and how many of them are just hanging around, desperately trying to feel like they are included in something. Whether it's a friendly old man wanting to pass the time of day, or a lonely person just wanting to feel like they're part of the human race, there is never a shortage of people trying to catch your eye and start a trivial and pointless conversation with you. People used to seek this kind of linkage in church. Now it's the nearest convenience store. They are also one of the few places where I am unable to avoid social interaction. For me, shopping is strictly business. All I want to do is select and pay for my goods, and get the fuck out of there before I have a panic attack, which is why I like frequenting this particular shop. Although I come here most days, and the staff all know my face well enough to try to establish some sort of rapport with me, they have never attempted to do so. Unfortunately, the man at the till today is new. I place the milk down on the counter, in between the chewing gums and the scratch cards.

"Morning," he says earnestly.

"Twenty Lambert and Butler, a packet of green Rizla and an ounce of Golden Virginia please."

I keep my eyes fixed firmly on the counter, but I can feel his eyes burrowing into the top of my head. He places the tobacco and cigarettes next to the milk.

"Anything else?"

18

I look up briefly, then straight back down at the counter as my eyes fleetingly meet his.

"Anything else mate?" he repeats.

"Nothing else," I say rummaging through the change in my pocket.

"Okee dokee mate, that'll be – "

But I don't need him to tell me. I know precisely how much it costs, and prepared the exact change before leaving my flat. I place the money down on the counter, grab my acquisitions and head for the door.

"You have a nice day too mate," I hear him shout sarcastically after me.

I know I have been a little rude, but if I had forced myself to engage in the man's pleasantries, I would be setting a bad precedent. The other staff here know not to bother making conversation with me, and he must learn this too if I am to continue shopping here. Tasks as simple as this can often fill me with anxiety, and even when conversing with people I know well, I can only bear a few seconds of eye contact at a time. I don't want anyone getting the wrong idea that I'm interested in being any part of their community.

This approach works. I know this because three days later I enter the shop again. The same man is behind the counter, but barely looks in my direction. He has clearly got the message, and is unlikely to bother me again.

This time, as I approach the counter a familiar face appears through the shop entrance. I could easily make it to the counter before them, but I hold back for a second and allow them to get there first. This isn't done as a polite gesture. This is someone who I've seen in the shop many times, and each time he has pushed in front of me. The reason I am yet to object is that, with his bulbous muscular frame, thickset neck, and a shaved head that looks as though it is made entirely of hardened fat, he resembles The Thing from The Fantastic Four, after a particularly heavy steroid binge.

The first time I was subjected to this gibbon's lack of etiquette, I was second in a fairly long queue, and he brazenly barged in front of me. As I was about to voice my objections, he turned around and looked down at me in a way that told me he wanted me to speak up, just to give him a reason to pummel me. I knew that if I dared utter a single syllable, it was very likely this man would gleefully assail me, if only to have a story to relate to his similarly un-evolved friends down at the gym, or wherever it is people like him congregate.

I knew that this could possibly be a defining moment in my life. *If I speak up now,* I thought to myself, *I risk incurring the wrath of a being slightly less evolved than Cro-Magnon man, but, by standing up for what is right, may gain the respect of everyone present, maybe even that of my primitive aggressor. Fuck, maybe I'd even gain a modicum of self-respect. He could smash my face in, or he could step aside and allow me free and unmolested passage to my rightful place at the front of the queue, and I will have set an important precedent, establishing myself as somebody not to be fucked with, somebody who is not willing to be pushed around or bullied by the likes of him.*

I opened my mouth to voice my objections, but the only sound I found myself capable of emitting was a pathetic, strangled croak. My throat felt dryer than the sands of the Mojave Desert, and I attempted to swallow to lubricate it. Still The Thing stared down at me, and laughed. In front of all those people. *The bastard fucking laughed at me.* I took a deep breath and attempted to speak once more. That time though, my natural cowardice ensured my silence. I looked down at the floor and The Thing turned away from me. An entire shop full of people witnessed my capitulation and now, every time I see this man in the shop, he pushes in front of me, knowing full well that I will say nothing.

FOUR

I open my eyes. I sleep on my back in the dead centre of my bed, so the first thing I see is the lampshade hanging from the ceiling. I crack the knuckles of each finger, starting with my right thumb, working along to the little finger, then switching to the little finger of my left hand and finishing with the left thumb. I put my feet down on the right side of the bed, letting my left foot touch down first, then lifting it back up, placing the right foot down, retracting it, then placing both feet down simultaneously. I stand in front of the mirror and check my body for blemishes, lesions or lumps. There is something near my left nipple. It could be a spot, but 400 men in the UK are diagnosed with breast cancer each year. There is every chance I could be one of them. I walk to the window and open the blinds, close them and then open them again. I leave my bedroom and turn left into the small spare room. After switching the light on and off seven times, I look around and make sure everything is in its place. There isn't much in there, just a small collection of books and CD's, a set of binoculars, my vacuum cleaner and a single chair, but I have to know they are exactly where I left them.

A left turn out of the spare room takes me into the kitchen. I turn on both taps, then open every cupboard door where all the food tins are stacked perfectly symmetrically, and with their labels facing out. I take them all out and replace them one by one, in reverse order to that in which they were removed. When I have finished, I turn off the taps and leave the kitchen.

Down the hall towards the front door is my bathroom. I go in and take the towel off the radiator, shake it out and then fold it back up and return it to the radiator. I open and close the shower curtain, open the window as wide as possible and walk from the bathroom to the front door. I unlock the door, then lock it again and walk across the hall to the living room. I take all the cushions off the couch and turn them over before I put them back, then rotate the coffee table 180 degrees, making sure the feet are placed down exactly within the indentations they had made in the carpet. If I am completely satisfied that everything is where it ought to be, I can begin my showering and dressing routine.

I walk back to the bathroom and switch on the shower.

While the water warms up I lay my clothes out on my bed, left to right, my boxer shorts near my pillow, T-shirt to the right, then my jeans, then my socks, with my shoes placed on the floor at the foot of the bed.

I walk back to the bathroom and lay a large towel on the floor next to the bath. I put the toilet seat down, and on top of it I place three folded towels, one for my hair, one for my torso and one for my legs.

When I have finished I put all the towels straight into the wash and walk back to my bedroom to get dressed. I move into my kitchen and switch on the kettle. While it boils I go back to the bathroom to take my morning medication.

This is my life. Every morning the same. A series of routines and rituals. It's all I have; these routines and this flat. These routines bring me comfort, this flat gives me security. I was 22 when I moved in, and I'm not sure I can envisage ever leaving. This place is perfect for me. It has its own front door, so although there are four other flats in the building, I need never come into contact with any of their occupants. In fact, I couldn't pick a single one of them out of a line-up. It is the one place I feel truly secure, the one place I have complete control over everything. The world outside seems dirty, scary and corrupt to me. It is an ugly place, and the vast majority of human beings that inhabit it are profoundly stupid people. But in here I am safe from all that, in here I am king.

FIVE

"Breathe in deeply through the nose. Hold the breath for a second, then breathe slowly out through the mouth. Repeat that a few times."

Brian is trying to teach me some breathing techniques that will help me to relax and to cope with stressful situations, and to deal with anxiety brought on by my O.C.D. I have long had my own coping mechanism for dealing with stress; what I call my "Rhythms", which involves twitching or tensing muscles or body parts in a certain order or rhythm. For example, I will tense the muscle in my right thigh, then in my left calf, followed by my right calf, and then finally my left thigh. I will then reverse this process twice, before finally repeating the first. I have equivalent systems for different sets of muscles or body parts. Although I will perform these rhythms at random times, they will often increase during moments of stress, and often act as a way for me to bring myself some sort of comfort and control in difficult situations. As well as these, I have been taking medication for a few years now in an attempt to control these compulsions, and also to control my general anxiety and depression. The dosages of these drugs have increased fairly rapidly. I am currently being prescribed 75mgs of Fluoxetine every morning, followed by 250mg of Quetiapine every evening. These are both very large dosages, but neither of them seems to be working particularly well. I am currently very near the guideline daily limit for both of my meds, and I think I will soon have to move up to those daily limits. If they fail to work then, I'm unsure where else there is for me to go. In an attempt to avoid increasing my dosages further, Brian has recently been focussing on different coping strategies, such as these breathing techniques.

"OK," I say, "so I do that three times?"

"Not necessarily three times."

"But you said a few times. A few usually means three."

"Just do it as many times as you feel is necessary Gary," Brian replies in a voice that is probably meant to be soothing, but which frankly irritates me slightly, "it can be once, it can be a hundred times, whatever you think you need."

"Right, well a hundred times is certainly significantly more

23

than a few isn't it? You need to be much clearer with your instructions Brian, you really should have just told me to repeat it as many times as I need in the first place. That would have avoided the confusion."

"Alright Gary, try not to focus on anything negative. Just concentrate on your breathing."

I attempt to purge my mind of all negative thoughts, I breathe deeply in the manner in which I have been instructed. I feel myself beginning to relax, but a thought still niggles away at me like a mosquito bite that demands to be scratched.

"You know Brian, if you're trying to show me a relaxation technique, it's probably advisable to demonstrate it in a way that won't simply serve to further agitate me."

Brian sits back down into his chair.

"Alright," he says, "let's talk about what in particular has made you angry since we last met."

"Just this fucking country," I sigh. "It's getting to the point where I can't step outside without something happening to make me angry."

"Can you give me an example?"

"What? Just the one? Ok; how about these pricks that walk around with their idiotic fucking music blaring out of their phones? Not even on headphones, just blasting out, assaulting the senses of anyone unlucky enough to be in the fucking vicinity. How about binge drinkers and happy slappers? How about these young mums shoving the corner of a Sayers pasty into their kid's mouths? How about Nick Clegg and Chris fucking Moyles? How about chain coffee shops, motorway service stations and all-night supermarkets? The EDL? Or the BNP and the cunts who vote for them? Or those vaguely studenty looking pretty boys and girls wearing those fucking vests, trying to guilt or seduce you into signing up for whichever fucking charity they represent? Is this not enough? You want some more fucking examples? Well then there's the fucking smog and pollution that fills your lungs and stings your eyes for a start, there's the footballers, the fascists, the fundamentalists and the fuckwits and the constant, unrelenting fucking noise. This country is fucked Brian, it is *fucked*. Somebody should just bomb this fucking nation into the dirt. Unleash the nuclear warheads, launch the biological weapons, let the missiles fly, and put us all out of our misery.

24

Seriously Brian? You live in this fucking country too, and you sit there and you ask me for *one* example? Well there's a few for fucking starters. This is what makes me angry, and, unless they can solve the intrinsic fucking deformities of this country's mindset, or at least those of this fucking town, no amount of breathing exercises that you can show me is going to make any fucking difference."

"Breathing exercises alone won't make much difference Gary. The main thing that will help you is a desire to let go of that kind of anger."

"What if I don't *want* to let go of my anger?" I ask.

"I thought the fact that we were practising these breathing exercises was indicative of the fact—"

"No," I interrupt, "we're practising these exercises to help me cope with stressful situations; you have just taken it for granted that I'm doing them as some form of anger management. At what point, Brian, have I ever said to you that I have a desire to rid myself of the kind of anger we're talking about? And I don't just mean today, I mean in the time that I've been coming to see you. When have I ever said that?"

"I suppose you never have," Brian concedes, "but, can I ask, why would you want to hold on to your anger? Anger is the most destructive of emotions."

"That's where you're wrong," I say, leaning forward in my chair, "anger is a greatly underrated emotion. It's just as valid as any other, and frankly, it's the only one I really value. Can I ask you a question Brian?"

"By all means."

"What if a man feels almost no emotion at all? He doesn't feel love, he doesn't feel sorrow, he doesn't feel any true joy, but the one thing, the *only* thing he does feel is anger. What if one were to take that away from him? What would be left then? Did you ever for one second during your arrogant, self-righteous attempts to rid me of my anger consider the possibility that I may want to hold on to it because quite often I feel as though it's the only fucking thing that actually makes me feel like I'm part of the human race? Did that possibility ever cross your mind while you were churning out the tired, lazy, unimaginative kind of therapy you learned at whatever second rate college you studied at?"

25

"OK," he says, barely concealing his annoyance with me, "have you been trying the exercise I asked you to do?"

The exercise Brian is referring to is something he suggested I try a few weeks ago. It simply involves the writing down of everything that annoys me or makes me angry. I am then supposed to read it all back to myself. The idea is that, upon reading it back, it won't seem as bad as when it initially angered me. Once I realise a matter isn't so bad, I can throw away the paper. This is supposed to symbolise me moving on from that particular issue.

"I've sort of been doing it, but I've adapted the process a little."

"Adapted it how?" Brian asks cautiously.

"Well, instead of just writing something down when it annoys me, I've been putting it in an email…"

"Ok…"

"..which I then send to the sports editor of the *Guardian*."

Brian looks at me silently for a few seconds.

"Why on earth would you send an email to the sports editor of the *Guardian*?"

"I thought it'd – "

"In fact, why on earth would you email these things to *anyone*? All I asked you to do was write down things that angered you, instead you appear to have embarked on a bizarre stalking exercise."

"Easy Brian, you're displaying signs of anger there. And it's such a destructive emotion. Do you want me to explain my motives?"

Brian, clearly becoming exasperated with me, gestures for me to continue.

"I thought it'd be an interesting way of expanding upon the theme. Instead of just writing down what angers me, I type it up in an email. Instead of throwing it away I send it to someone."

"But….why the sports editor of the *Guardian*?"

"Well, I'd sent him an email a few days before you set me this exercise to do. I was complaining about the poor grammar in an article I'd read about the runner Steve Cram. My email was neither published nor replied to, so I was pretty pissed off with him to begin with. Plus I think anyone who gets paid for writing about nothing but sport has it far too easy anyway, so he just

26

seemed like the obvious candidate."

Brian is gripping his notebook as though he wants to hit me with it, and looks like he's silently counting to ten; another of his unoriginal anger management techniques .

"OK. That's... fine. It's certainly not what I had asked you to do but... fine. So what did you write about?"

"Mainly two-abreast."

"Two-abreast?"

"Yeah. Earlier that day I'd had to get the train somewhere."

"Where were you going?"

"That's irrelevant," I say dismissively, "I always hate getting the train anyway, they're squalid, claustrophobic and unclean, so having to get one usually puts me in a disagreeable mood to begin with. On the escalators on the way down to the platform there was a young couple in front of me. They were standing two-abreast with their arms round each other so I couldn't get past them. Everyone knows that you should keep to the right on escalators. Because of them holding me up I just missed my train and had to wait fifteen minutes for the next one."

"And you didn't think to excuse yourself past them?"

"Oh yeah, coz it's really that fucking simple for someone like me. I think you know me better than that by now."

"True. Was there anything else?"

"There was actually. After I had finally got off the train I was walking home. I turned onto the main road that my street is off and this time there's an elderly couple walking right in front of me, shuffling along taking up the entire pavement so once again I'm being held up. The road we were on is very busy so I couldn't step onto it to overtake them so instead I had to walk even slower than this decrepit pair of old puffins. I could have been late for a very important meeting for all they knew. It's just downright inconsiderate of people."

Brian thinks for a moment and makes a few notes in his pad.

"I don't think it's the lack of consideration that really bothered you."

"No? Then what was it?"

"I think it's interesting that both of the incidents you've just mentioned involved people in couples. I think you felt angry not by the delay these couples caused you, but by the fact that it seemed to you as though they were shoving their love in your

27

face somehow."

"My word, you've really outdone yourself in terms of predictability this time. A ten year old could have done better; that's got nothing to do with it. It just annoys me. It wouldn't have made any difference to me if it'd been two friends. It's the fact that they were getting in my way, the complete lack of consideration that bothers me. What you're saying is, as usual, bollocks."

"I don't think it is bollocks. I couldn't help but notice the contemptuous way you said the word 'couple'. When talking about the train station you emphasised that they were a young couple, therefore this is a couple at the start of a romance, with all the excitement and discoveries that entails. You then described the second couple as being elderly. Therefore this is a couple whose love has endured probably over decades, and who still have the kind of companionship which you have been denied."

"I've been denied nothing. My single status is one that I have chosen, not one that has been forced upon me."

"Yes, but that's still denial. Self denial maybe, but the fact remains you have been denied the companionship that these people clearly cherish, and I strongly believe that this is what is at the core of many of your problems. It's no coincidence that the intensity of your O.C.D. has increased in direct correlation with the amount of time you've been single."

Brian waits for me to respond, but I can't think of anything to say. I look at my watch. It shows five minutes of the session remaining.

"Can I go?" I ask after nearly a minute's silence.

"You're free to leave any time you like," Brian says.

While I'm putting my coat on, I turn back to Brian.

"I'm not leaving because you've touched a nerve. I'm leaving because, if that kind of by-the-numbers, hackneyed analysis is all you've got to offer, it's a waste of my time being here."

As I get to the door the sound of Brian's voice stops me.

"Just one other thing…"

"What is it Columbo?"

"I was just wondering, when you send all these emails to the *Guardian*, doesn't he just block your email address or

28

something?"

"Yeah, but I just set up a different address each time I send him one. That way it doesn't matter if he blocks me."

Brian smiles almost imperceptibly.

"See you next week," he says.

As my bus home approaches, I quickly assess that it is over 75% full, so rather than have to sit next to some complete stranger and run the risk of them trying to make conversation with me, I wave it past and decide to walk home from this week's session. After about fifteen minutes I come to a busy crossing. As the traffic shows no signs of abating I reach out to press the button on the traffic lights. Just millimetres away from it, however, I stop. Staring at the tiny little white button I wonder how many grubby fingers have come into contact with it before. I think of the people who, in their thousands, pass by here every day, and the thought of touching something so many of them have touched before is too hideous to contemplate. Usually in this situation I would pull my sleeve down and push the button, but today I think of the microbes and germs getting onto my clothing, burying themselves deep in the fibres, and from there passing onto my skin, my furniture, my light switches and door handles. This seems at least as bad as direct skin contact, so I decide to endure the smoggy fumes for as long as it takes till the traffic dies down or the lights change of their own accord.

I stare straight ahead, watching car after car speed past me. After a while, the passing traffic becomes hypnotic, flying past almost in a blur. I imagine what would happen if I simply stepped off the kerb. With this high a volume of traffic travelling at these speeds, death would probably be instantaneous. I don't seriously consider doing it; I've never been suicidal, although I often think it would be better if I had simply never existed, it just occurs to me that a quick and mostly painless death at this point wouldn't be a bad thing. The mess I would leave behind, however, is an unsettling thought. Lost in these thoughts, I barely notice a man in a wheelchair pulling up beside me. I am in between the wheelchair user and the traffic lights so there is no way he can reach the button. Even if I wasn't there he'd probably struggle. Out of the corner of my eye, I see him arching his neck to see the little electronic red man, signifying that the button has not yet been pressed. My worst fears are confirmed when he looks up at me.

"Excuse me mate." I turn and look down to see a middle aged man with a friendly face. "Could you press the button for me please?"

I have to think on my feet now. How do I manage to avoid both touching the button and causing offence to a disabled person?

"It's alright, the lights will probably change soon anyway."

This really is the best I can come up with. It is now imperative that the lights change. As the traffic continues to flow, and the lights show no sign of changing, it is clear that things are not going to be that simple for me.

"I don't think the lights are gonna change mate," the man says to me, "these ones never seem to change unless you actually press the button. Do you think you could do it for me please? I've got a bit of a height disadvantage here."

He gestures towards his wheelchair and laughs, but I'm far too tense to share in the joke. I look at the friendly, plaintive face of the man and back at the dirty, germ ridden button he's imploring me to press. I wish I could help him but I can practically see the microbes and germs swimming around on there. I wonder who designed these lights, who installed them. I wonder whose decision it was to set them to activate so infrequently, and whether they have any idea of the pain and stress their dilatory, myopic decisions cause for other people, most notably me. I curse the town planners, the programmers, the decision makers and the button pushers whose stupidity and imprudence had left me floundering here, in this septic fucking town, at these bastard fucking traffic lights with their rancid fucking button, with this friendly fucking man who I cannot help by performing the most basic of fucking tasks.

"Is there a problem?" he asks me.

"Well no..." I mumble, too embarrassed to admit what's really wrong, "it's just, is it really so urgent that I press the button?"

"I am in a bit of a hurry, it would be a big help to me if you could."

I wish he wasn't so bloody polite, then it would be much easier for me to refuse to perform such a simple favour for him. I look at his wheelchair again, and it occurs to me that I could explain to him why I'm hesitating. This man has a disability and I, in a sense, have one too. I wouldn't dare to compare my problems to his, but his predicament could make him more sympathetic than most people. But I know I don't have the communication skills to put this across without sounding like an idiot.

"Look," I say, "I'm sure that whatever it is you're trying to get to can't really be that important."

"I beg your pardon? I hope you're not implying that my plans aren't as important as yours, just because I'm in a wheelchair? Disabled people do have social engagements too you know mate."

The man's tone remains civil, but this situation is now very delicately poised, and I'm going to have to work hard to ensure it doesn't turn ugly.

"No, of course not. What I mean is, the few seconds you may have to wait here if I don't press the button surely won't make any real difference to you in the overall course of your day will they?"

"Does this mean you won't press the button?"

"Not so much that I *won't* press it, it's just that it'd be a lot easier for me if I didn't have to."

"Is this some sort of joke?" he asks, genuinely perplexed.

"No, no joke. I just..." I look round and see no one else is within earshot, then crouch down a little to confide in him. "I just really, *really* can't press that button."

"Why not?"

"The germs!" I say. "Think of the germs!"

"What germs?"

"The germs of thousands of people, all pushing that same button with their grubby little fingers. God knows what they could have been doing. They could have just scratched their arses or picked their noses. They could have been picking up their dog's shit seconds before crossing this road. They may even have some sort of hideous disease which can be passed on by touch, *you just don't know*! This button could be riddled with Rotavirus, Streptococcus or Staphylococcus. Some viruses can survive on surfaces like that for up to 72 hours."

"Is there something wrong with you?"

31

I realise I've become a little too intense, so I take a step back and try to regain some composure.

"There's nothing wrong with me, it's just that – "

"Well," the man interrupts, "if there's nothing wrong with you then you can press the button can't you?"

He's losing patience with me now, and I don't blame him. I turn to the button again and reach out to push it. Once again I get within millimetres of it, but I know already that, especially under this kind of pressure, I'm not going to be able to touch it. I pause with my finger extended for about half a minute. I turn back to the wheelchair user. His face is now red with anger.

"JUST PRESS THE BUTTON YOU FUCKING WEIRDO! *DO IT NOW FREAK!*" he yells, eyes and neck veins bulging with rage. It seems that it takes only a couple of minutes in my company to turn a polite, friendly person into a foul mouthed aggressor, ready to explode with violence at any second.

"I can't do it," I whimper, "I'm sorry, I just can't do it."

And with that I dart between the onrushing traffic, across the busy road and away, the distant voice of the disabled man still yelling abuse at me.

As I approach my flat I notice my parents getting out of their car. This is an unexpected and frankly unwelcome visit.

My parents' names are Paul and Janet. They are both in their mid-60s, and both are semi-retired teachers. They met about 40 years ago when my mum got a job as an English teacher in the school where my dad was teaching history. They married two years later and ten months after that my brother was born.

Mum and Dad are typical lower-middle class baby-boomer liberals. The type that managed to rebel in a half-hearted way in the 60s, and yet still become reasonably affluent through the 80s and 90s. Their youthful forays into the anti-capitalist movement apparently gave them enough knowledge of the capitalist system to be able to exploit it over the ensuing decades, and they seem to believe that making regular contributions to various charities by Direct Debit redresses the balance. I suppose I give my parents a pretty hard time. I think they are convinced that I blame them for the way I am, but I don't. They never really did very much wrong as parents; they just happened to give birth to an anomaly. Mum and Dad also think I hate them. I'm not sure whether or not this is the case, but our relationship is certainly fraught. Brian once asked me if I love my parents, to which, in order to be completely honest, I had to answer that I didn't. I said I can't love my parents or anyone else, because I don't think I have any understanding of what love is, or any capability of feeling it.

"Alright son," my Dad says as I walk towards them. I can tell from his tone of voice that they've come to deliver what they consider to be bad news.

"I'm afraid we've got some bad news for you," says Mum, confirming my suspicions. I take them up to the flat and we sit down in the lounge. My mum and dad both have this odd solemn look on their faces. They both stare down at the floor, not saying anything. After the experience I've just had, I'm impatient for them to get to the point so I can get them out and be on my own. Also, the snooker is on TV and I'd like to be able to watch it uninterrupted.

"So are you actually going to tell me what this bad news is or am I expected to guess?"

My mum makes a gesture to my dad for him to tell me.

"We got a phone call this morning, and I'm afraid that your uncle Mickey passed away last night."

Uncle Mickey is (or was) my dad's elder brother. We haven't seen him since I was in school. He moved down south with his wife years ago. He was close to the family when I was younger but after he moved we lost touch. Even Dad only heard from him about once a year. I search for some memories of him. I remember him having a beard and looking like Mathew Kelly. He used to take me and Ben to the match when we were kids, but since then I've not really thought about him at all.

"Are you OK?" asks Mum.

"I'm absolutely fine."

Silence. It would seem that my parents were expecting more of a reaction, but the death means nothing to me. We're talking about someone I haven't seen since I was a child and whose name is hardly even mentioned anymore. Besides, the thing that is foremost in my mind at present is the incident at the traffic lights, and the fact that I need to be alone to recover from it.

"Don't you want to know how he died?" Mum asks quietly. I can't believe she'd ask such a ridiculous question.

"Of course I don't want to know how he died. What fucking

difference does that make?"

"Gary, he was your uncle." My dad seems hurt and angered by my lack of interest.

"Dad, we haven't seen him in about fourteen years. He hasn't been part of any of our lives for that long, so it makes no difference to any of us that he's dead now."

"How can you say that?" my Mum asks tearfully. "He loved you and your brother; you used to go to the football with him all the time." I'm getting impatient now; I need to get these people out of here.

"I'm not disputing those things Mum. I'm just saying that he's been out of the picture for some time, so nothing has really changed for any of us. There's no actual impact on any of our lives. And as for you being so desperate to reveal the manner of his death, well I just find that a bit ghoulish. There's nothing to be gained from me knowing how he died, other than to satisfy morbid curiosity, which I simply do not have. How dare you come round uninvited like this and try to play games with me."

"Play games? What do you mean play games? Me and your mum just thought you'd want to know the news, that's all," my Dad says.

"Don't give me that shit. You could have just phoned me. We all know why you really came round here today. You wanted to see how I'd react. You're fucking testing me. You're thinking that it's been so long since either of you saw me display any real emotion, or actually get upset about anything, that you wanted to know whether someone's death could bring anything out of me. You were wondering if the news of poor old Uncle Mickey's untimely demise would touch me so deeply that my stoical façade would crack and I'd collapse in a fit of tears. Well I'm sorry to disappoint you, but that isn't going to happen. I'm not going to pretend to be heartbroken just because it's what people expect of me. And yes Dad, he was my uncle, but he was your brother. And you had barely made any effort to contact him for over a decade. So what does that say about you? Don't try and make yourself feel better about your shortcomings as a brother by taking the moral high ground over the fact that I won't shed a tear. Don't be such a fucking hypocrite."

My Dad gets up from the couch.

"Come on Jan, I think it's best if we just go."

"Yes I think that's an excellent fucking idea. And in future I'd appreciate it if you didn't make these unannounced visits."

"Unannounced visits?" Mum asks. "Are we supposed to make appointments with you now?"

"Yes actually, you are. In future, don't come round here without a fucking appointment. If you want to see me, you can ring me well in advance. In fact, fuck that, don't ring me, it's far too fucking personal, you can send me a fucking email *requesting* that I grant you an appointment."

MymMum is trying to fight back the tears now, and my dad ushers her through my front door and down the stairs.

"Come on Jan, let's just go," he says, putting a reassuring arm around her shoulder, "you know there's no talking to him when he gets like this."

"On second thoughts just don't fucking bother contacting me at all," I yell down the stairs as I slam the door closed behind them. As they walk down the path towards their car I overhear my mum speaking to my dad from my window.

"I don't know where the hell we went wrong with that boy."

SIX

"What do you get out of these sessions?"

"It's not about what I get from them Gary, these sessions are designed to help you."

This week's session with Brian isn't going particularly well. Sometimes I just can't hide my contempt for the therapy process. Today is one of those days and, unfortunately for Brian, I am taking it out on him.

"Ostensibly they are designed to help me, but there must be something in it for you, other than the extortionate amount of money you get paid."

"Gary," Brian says using that patronising tone of his, the tone that is meant to calm and relax me, but always has the opposite effect of making my blood boil, "my feelings are irrelevant to what we—"

"I never said it was relevant," I interrupt, "I know it's not fucking relevant. I don't give a fuck whether or not it's fucking relevant. I just happen to be curious as to what you gain from the dozens of hours you must waste every week talking to me and however many other losers and freaks sit in this same chair. Personally I think you're a bit fucking sick Brian."

"How so?" Asks Brian, suddenly a bit less interested in whether or not this line of conversation is relevant.

"Well I can only assume you get off on it somehow. I mean, I imagine the stuff we talk about is pretty fucking prosaic and mundane compared with some of the salacious shit you must hear every day. I mean, you must have people tell you about all kinds of weird sex stuff for example. Is that it? Is that the attraction? What do you do Brian, wait for some girl who's been sexually abused, then get her to describe it in lurid, explicit detail so you can go home and crack one off over it? I bet you secretly record the sessions with the sex freaks don't you? You've probably got a vast library of tapes of girl's detailing the most bizarre sexual depravities imaginable, and every night you go home, tell your wife you've got some work to do, then lock yourself away in your study, put on a pair of headphones, and spend the entire night masturbating. Is that what you do? It is, isn't it you fucking sick old bastard? You disgusting fucking pervert."

"I know what you're trying to do Gary," he says in that same tone, "you're trying to embarrass me. You're trying to embarrass me, and it's a distraction technique, so that you can avoid talking about the real issues here."

"Well maybe the real issue for me today is you, and what you are."

"And what am I?" he asks.

"You're an emotional rapist Brian. You get inside people heads, uninvited – "

"I am never uninvited, the people who come to see me seek me out for help."

"I NEVER SOUGHT YOU OUT!" Brian recoils slightly at the volume of my voice, finally shaken out of his placidity. "I was sent here, I never invited anyone inside my head. I never fucking wanted anyone in my head. But you get deep inside there don't you Brian? Not just with me, but with everyone you talk to. You get in there amongst all the shit and the pain and the guilt and the secrets, all those places that nobody should ever be allowed into, and you derive whatever fucking pleasure you do from it, then you move on to the next person. You're an emotional and mental rapist."

"I don't think this kind of talk is helpful to you in the slightest Gary. Like I said before, my feelings are irrelevant. What is important and what is relevant is you, and how you are feeling."

"BUT THAT'S JUST IT, ISN'T IT BRIAN," this time I'm not just shouting, but am actually on my feet, "THAT'S THE WHOLE FUCKING POINT! I *DON'T* FEEL. I'M JUST NUMB. SOMETIMES I'LL FEEL ANGRY, SOMETIMES I'LL FEEL ANXIOUS, BUT MOSTLY I'M JUST FUCKING *NUMB*!"

I collapse back into my chair. We sit in silence for a few moments. Brian knows by now, after these rants, just to leave me for a short while until I've calmed down. It takes about five minutes for that to happen. I look across at Brian. Rather than looking at me, he's looking away from me at the farthest corner of the room. This is another thing he knows to do at times like this, as being stared at would send me back into my outburst.

"I'm sorry about that," I say. I'm not sure how sincere my apology is, or whether I should really have issued it. In some ways, I think this kind of outburst is a natural occupational hazard for someone like Brian. If you choose to earn your living by talking to disturbed and mentally ill people, the least you should expect is to get shouted at.

"No apologies necessary Gary. We've been in this situation more than enough times for me to understand."

This comment irks me somewhat. I'm offended by the implication that he and I share some sort of camaraderie, as though we've stood shoulder to shoulder on the battlefield of life, simply by virtue of the fact that Brian listens to me moan for an hour a week. On another day, this may have provoked another tirade, but I'm spent after this last one, so I decide to let it go this time.

"Right, whatever. I don't really think those things about you Brian. Well not all of them anyway."

I may have been a little unfair on Brian, but I know why I felt driven to attack him like that. I want him to realise that he is not in control of these sessions. He probably only has to use a few big words or quote something from a psychology handbook to impress most of the dimwits he speaks to. Their lack of intelligence is what puts him in control, but he doesn't have the same advantage over me, and I want to make sure he knows that.

Brian puts his notebook on the arm of his chair and walks over to the window. He stands there for a few minutes in silence.

"OK," he says finally.

"Is everything alright Brian?" I ask.

He doesn't answer me. He exhales deeply and walks back to his chair, where he sits with his hands folded under his chin. I'm unsure whether this is some sort of new technique of his, or whether he has something on his mind.

"Brian, if this is a new therapeutic method you've developed, it's not really working. I don't know if you're expecting me to talk or what. I mean, I know I'm not actually paying for these sessions, so I don't give a shit if we sit here in silence for an hour, but it seems like a bit of a waste of time."

"I've been thinking a lot about you over the last few weeks Gary."

"Ok. Can't say I reciprocate, but... fine."

"And about our sessions."

"What about them?"

"I've been wondering whether they're actually doing you any good. Whether coming here for an hour a week and talking to me is actually having any kind of positive impact on your life."

"And what conclusions have you come to?" I ask.

"The conclusion I've come to Gary is that, quite frankly, I don't think they are doing you any good whatsoever."

"I see. So what are you trying to tell me? Are you saying you want me to go to another therapist?"

"No. I'm saying that I think therapy as a whole is doing you no good. I think as long as you're in therapy, it'll be a convenient excuse for you not to challenge yourself. Let me ask you a very simple yes or no question Gary. Do you want to get better?"

"Well first of all Brian, that is far from a 'simple yes or no question'. If you genuinely think that there is a single question concerning the human psyche that can be answered with a monosyllabic response, then you should be struck off and never be allowed near mentally-ill people again. Besides which, I have no concept of what 'getting better' could possibly entail. The way I am is the only way I really know. If you're asking me if, were it somehow possible, I could click my fingers and make all my issues disappear, if I would do it, then I don't know. I don't know if I could cope with normality. I'm mad. I know that. But I am, in some way, comfortable with it. To have my mental illness removed would rid me of the one thing about myself that has ever been consistent. Of course, what you're asking me is the most stupid of hypothetical questions."

"Right. That's what I thought you'd say."

"Brian, I'm not sure exactly what the point you're trying to make is, but please do me the courtesy of not talking in riddles and just spelling it the fuck out for me."

"Alright then. I've decided to do something that you may consider quite radical, but that I consider to be completely necessary for you to progress."

"Which is what exactly?" I ask anxiously.

"I've decided that I'm going to report that you are no longer unfit for work, and recommend that you immediately be taken off all incapacity benefits and find work."

"WHAT?!?!?" I feel like I have been punched in the stomach. Either Brian has become a sadist, or this is some sort of cruel prank he's playing on me.

"Now I know you may be a little upset –"

"Upset?" I interrupt. "Up-*fucking*-set? That's an understatement don't you think? Why the fuck have you decided to do this? Is this some kind of fucking target thing? Do you get paid some fucking fat bonus for getting people like me off the dole? Massaging the fucking stats a bit, is that it?"

"I'm doing this because I think it's the best possible thing for you. Our sessions aren't doing you any good. Every week you come here I see you becoming more and more detached from the world around you. Yes, you are given the opportunity to express and unburden yourself, but you are not making any progress. You need to get out of the rut you're in and get back into the real world, and it's crystal clear that you'll never make that jump of your own volition, so I've decided to give you a little push."

"Brian, please don't do this to me, I'm not ready. You're throwing me to the fucking wolves. As hopelessly fucking incompetent as you are, even you must realise this is a ludicrous course of action. Surely you can see how irresponsible—"

"What would be irresponsible would be for me to allow you to continue to wallow in this perpetual state of anger and isolation. You need to be around other people. Having a job will increase your self-esteem considerably, it'll be an easy way to meet people and it'll break up the stifling routines and rituals you immerse yourself in."

"You....you fucking......QUACK!" I yell. "You fucking bastard shrink! How can you do this to me?"

Despite my aggressive manner, Brian's imperturbable countenance doesn't drop for a second.

"If you think you can intimidate or guilt me into changing my mind, you're very much mistaken. I've thought long and hard about this Gary, it's not a decision I've taken lightly, and I honestly believe that it would be a dereliction of duty on my part to not attempt this. I'm not saying it's going to be easy for you, I know it's going to be difficult, and I know what a big deal this is for you, but I do think it's the best course of action, and who knows, you might even come to enjoy being in full time employment."

"I seriously fucking doubt that."

"You'll still be able to contact me and we can schedule

sessions if you feel you need them."

"Oh what's the fucking point Brian? You said yourself they achieve nothing, I haven't progressed one single fucking iota since I started coming here. They've basically been a complete fucking waste of time."

"I never said they've been—"

"Oh just fucking save it Brian, I've heard enough. Why don't you just admit it? You're giving up on me, it's that simple."

"Gary," Brian protests, "I am not giving up on you."

"It's OK," I say, "I can't say that I blame you. I mean, I'm a complete fucking hopeless case. I've known it all along, and you probably have too. I suppose now you feel like you've put enough time into me, time that could be better used for someone else who isn't a total write-off, and you've decided it's time to give up on me."

"The only person who's given up on you Gary," he says, still unshaken by my demeanour, "is yourself."

I stand up and lean right into Brian's face.

"You fucking idiot. You cunt. You fucking stupid, fat, complacent, hypocritical fucking bastard. What you're doing will probably fucking destroy me, Brian. Why don't you just put a fucking bullet through my head and be done with it? Fuck you Brian. Fuck you and your entire fucking profession."

I storm out of the office, slamming the door behind me. I walk out onto the street, more frightened than I have ever been in my life.

I make my way back to my flat in a daze and, in response to the agitated text messages I sent them on my way, Jimmy, Darren and Aimee have all come round to offer their moral support. These are the only three friends I have not managed to alienate. I met Darren and Aimee while we were all attending the same secondary school, and Darren and Aimee became boyfriend and girlfriend within weeks. They've been together ever since and married two years ago. They visit me once every week or so, probably as much out of some misguided sense of duty as friendship. I think they are labouring under the misapprehension that I somehow need them to visit me, and that without their support and friendship I would be unable to cope, and this offends me. I have no problem with them coming to visit me, as

41

long as it is on my terms, but if I never saw them again, I doubt that it would really have that much of an impact on my life.

Jimmy has been friends with us since Darren and I went to college. Jimmy now works as a website designer for some sort of fashion or music magazine. Or is it a fashion *and* music magazine? He's told me a hundred times but I don't think I've ever been interested enough to remember. He recently "came out of the closet", which came as a great surprise to us all, given that he was the only one from our circle of friends to have had regular girlfriends, and since then I've seen him less and less as he is revelling in his new found gayness, visiting gay bars and clubs and having an alarming number of one night stands with as many strangers as he can find. I don't know any more details about Jimmy's sex/social life, and don't want to. I'm not a homophobe, I just find the idea of homosexuality perplexing. The thought of a man and a woman copulating is odd enough, but the thought of two men fucking each other just seems ludicrous.

I suppose they're decent enough people (whatever that means), but every time they visit, I constantly find myself looking at my watch, wondering when they will leave, especially when Darren and Aimee begin talking to each other in those ludicrous, child-like voices that people always seem to adopt when they become part of a couple. It's something I have never understood, and have always found slightly unsettling.

"Well, maybe it will be good for you. You know, getting out there, meeting people, all that shit," is Jimmy's predictable perspective.

"Yeah man," continues Darren, "who knows? It's worth a try though isn't it?"

I should have known better than to expect anything else from these people. I feel like I'm about to have a fucking brain haemorrhage, and all they can offer are useless trite remarks. They can't begin to imagine the momentousness of what is about to happen to me, so I shouldn't be surprised that their advice is so uninventive.

"They could be right Gary," offers Aimee, "I can't remember you ever having a job, and there are worse things in the world than actually earning a living – "

"As opposed to what?" I ask, "Sponging off the state?
42

Bleeding the economy dry and taking from decent, hard-working tax payers like you?"

"No, she didn't mean it like that mate," says Darren, trying to placate me.

"Don't tell me what I did or didn't mean, Darren. Frankly Gary, yes, that's exactly what I mean." Aimee apparently doesn't share her husband's desire to placate me. "How long do you plan to continue living like this? You're not a bloody kid anymore. You're approaching thirty and it's about time you started acting like it. So what if you've got to work? Big fucking deal. Everyone else has to do it, so why shouldn't you? Do you think I like going to work? I can assure you I don't. Darren doesn't like having to get up at six o'clock every morning to drive for an hour to get to work. Nobody likes going to work, but it's what happens in the real world."

"Thanks for the advice Aimee, and thanks for framing it in such a condescending way, but your over-simplification of the matter shows a deep lack of understanding of my condition and the impact such a change as this is likely to have on me."

"Who's being condescending now? It's not that I don't understand, it's just that I'm sick of tip-toeing around you and making excuses for you. You seem to live your life under the assumption that you are the most important person in the world. Do you think you're the only person who has problems? Or the only person who has O.C.D.? Thousands of people go out to work and lead productive lives despite having far worse problems than you do. It's about fucking time you developed a work ethic."

Having a work ethic is a quality I've always considered to be vastly overrated, and have never understood why some people place such importance on it, as though being a compliant worker bee is an admirable character trait. Personally I am proud not to possess a work ethic, but I decide it would be futile to argue the point, and instead allow Aimee to kid herself that she has had an original thought.

"You're completely self-absorbed Gary."

"Yeah. And?"

"What do you mean 'and'?" You don't think there's anything wrong with being selfish and self-absorbed?"

"I have no opinion either way on whether it's a good thing or a bad thing. My point is, me being self-absorbed doesn't affect

43

you or anyone else. I'm not married. I don't share my home with anyone. I barely even share my time with anyone. So I can be as self-absorbed as I like. And I'm not selfish. To be selfish, one has to pursue one's own pleasure or gratification at the expense of others. Because I live alone, my lifestyle and the way I act has no impact on anyone else."

"Gary, you are selfish. You're the most selfish person I have ever known. And it's the kind of selfishness that comes from assuming you're the most important person on the planet. Well maybe one day you'll learn that you aren't the most important... there are more important things..." she trails off mid-sentence.

"OK, I think you've made your point." Darren has taken pity on me and saved me from further admonishment, putting his arms round Aimee's shoulders and sitting her back down. "Well anyway, no matter what any of us think," he says calmly while his wife continues to seethe next to him, "the fact is that you've got to find work now, so you should probably think about what kind of work you'd like to do."

"Christ, I have no idea. Something with as little human contact as possible I suppose."

"Doesn't that defeat the object though?" asks Jimmy.

"Yeah well, it's not my objective; it's that fat fucker Brian's. But I suppose I'll just have to see what kind of interviews I get sent to."

"Look," says Jimmy after a moment's silence, "if you really don't want to work that much, you can always just shit your pants before going into every interview and make sure you answer every question with a stream of swear words; nobody wants to employ an incontinent man with Tourette's Syndrome."

We all laugh and the tension in the room drops slightly. Darren turns to Aimee.

"Why don't we tell him now?"

"No, maybe now's not the best time."

"It's as good a time as any," he replies.

"Tell me what?" I ask.

"No it's OK, it can wait."

"Aimee, whatever it is, I'm so intrigued now that it can't possibly wait. What is it?"

"Well alright then, I was gonna wait to tell you but if you insist. The news is that I'm pregnant."

44

"Fuck!" Is the only response I can come up with. This explains her comments about "most important person on the planet".

"Fuck? Is that all you can say?" she asks angrily.

"No, no, I didn't mean it like that. It's just a shock, but a great one," I manage to muster up some enthusiasm from somewhere. Darren and Aimee are the type of young modern couple who attempt to live a lifestyle as environmentally friendly as possible. They recycle everything, and buy as many recycled products as they can. If they had informed me of their intentions to start a family at any other time, I would have pointed out how this goes against their lifestyle, and that having a child is the single most damaging thing they could do to the environment, in terms of the amount of energy, food, and various other products that will be consumed by a child. I would point out that if they really wanted to limit their impact on the environment, they would have made a conscious decision not to have any children a long time ago, and I would ask them whether they are sincere in their desire to save the environment, or whether, as I have always suspected, it is merely an affectation of the type people like them are prone to. Given the current circumstances though, I think better of it.

"Really, congratulations," I say shaking their hands.

I sit back down and look at the few friends I have in the world. I look at Jimmy, a man who's had more girlfriends than anyone I know; now embarking upon life as a gay man. A lifestyle I may not be 100% comfortable with, but one that he's thrown himself into with reckless abandon. I look at Aimee and Darren, not only getting on with their own lives, but about to bring a new life into the world. All around me real life is happening, and I've been stuck in my little cocoon trying to deny there is even a world outside it. I've been standing still for years, but the world has still been spinning. And now, like it or not, I am to be forced to spin with it.

SEVEN

The girl behind the counter drops the change into my hand; a collection of both silver and copper coins. Some of these coins have been in circulation for twenty years or more, and will have been handled by untold thousands of people so, without closing my hand, I carefully open my pocket with my spare hand, and deftly drop the coins in, ensuring they have only minimal contact with my skin. When I get home, it will be necessary to wash my hands, and clean the coins before I have to handle them again. Any germs living on the coins could have been transferred to the inside of my pocket, so I will wash my jeans too, just to be on the safe side.

Stepping out of the door, I'm almost knocked over by a man running past me. As he speeds by, I notice that he has what is unmistakably a blob of shit on his ear.

"The bastards. The fucking dirty bastards," he yells at nobody in particular. Another man passing by shouts to him.

"What happened mate?"

Without slowing down, the first man points in the direction of Balls Road East.

"Some filthy fucking twat rubbed dog shit on the fucking pay phone."

He carries on running and disappears down Slatey Road. The second man turns to me.

"This fucking place," he says. "In any other town, that would seem shocking."

I have to nod in agreement, before I walk away, reading the morning newspaper as I go. Because I am not paying full attention to where I'm going, I accidentally knock shoulders with another man on the pavement. I apologise without looking up from my paper and carry on walking.

"Gary?" I hear him say. I turn around to face him, but am surprised when I don't recognise him.

"Gary Lennon?" he asks. "It is you isn't it?"

I stare at the man, trying hard to place him, but coming up short.

"Do I know you?" I ask eventually. This unexpected interaction has put me instantly on edge, and I can feel a panic attack looming

"Of course you do, it's me, Derek. Derek Oliver." The name rings a bell, but I can't think straight.

"We were in school together."

Now it comes back to me a little. If I remember rightly, we were in the same maths class for the first two years of secondary school. I don't remember very much about him, other than a vague memory that he had a sinus problem, which caused him to have a constantly running nose, and a permanent layer of dried, crusty snot on his top lip, which led to the inevitable nickname of Snotty Oliver. I don't recall disliking him particularly, but nor do I recall us being what one would call "friends".

"Oh right, yeah. I remember now." I have nothing to say to him, so I briefly acknowledge him, and then turn to walk away.

"So how the hell are you mate?" Derek says, stopping me before I've even walked a few steps. I turn back to him.

"I'm fine, thanks."

There follows a pause during which Derek looks at me expectantly. In situations like this, I often forget the basic pleasantries that come so naturally to other people. It's partly because I'm out of practice, and partly because I simply have no interest in making small talk with someone I haven't seen since school.

"And how are you?" I ask reluctantly.

"Fantastic mate, still working at the bank" – Still? Does he think I already know this? – "and I got married last year too."

"Congratulations," I say without enthusiasm or sincerity.

"What about you? Are you married or anything, where are you working these days?"

"I'm neither working nor married," I deadpan.

"Ah well, I'm sure something will come up, on both counts. What type of work are you interested in? Maybe I can put in a word for you down at the bank or something."

What is this guy's problem? Can he not determine from my attitude, and the brevity of my answers, that I do not want to continue this conversation? And what in the name of God would make him think that I would, for one second, even consider the possibility of working in a bank? Or for that matter, that any bank manager would consider me a suitable employee? If he isn't going to take the hint, I will have to use more direct tactics,

47

otherwise I could be stuck here talking to this person for days.

"Listen... erm... Derek," I say, barely remembering his name, "I'm in a bit of a hurry at the moment, so – "

"Ok, fair enough mate." I'm relieved to hear him say this, and I begin to turn away. I am distraught, therefore, to see him reaching into his pocket and pulling out his mobile phone. "Tell you what, why don't we swap numbers? Or you can just send me a message on Facebook. Then we can go out for a drink sometime and catch up."

Jesus Christ. Are people really this fucking stupid? Why on earth would I want to catch up with this man? What have we got to catch up over? I've spent most of the last decade trying to avoid situations like this, and I imagine that he has already told me the most interesting facts of his life. Why will he not get the message and let me go? Does he not realise the suffering he is causing?

"Look Derek," I say in the most placating voice I can manage, "I'd rather not swap numbers with you to be honest."

"Why not?" He's genuinely puzzled.

"I just... don't really have the time or the room in my life for new friends."

"But I'm not a new friend," he actually seems to be deeply hurt by this, "I'm an old friend, we go way back."

"Yes!" I exclaim. "Exactly! *WAY* back, way back into the past, that was when we were friends, years and years ago. Let's face it Derek, if there was any reason for us to have stayed in touch, we would have done so and there would be no need for us to exchange numbers. Now I really don't want to offend you, but I think it's probably best if we just go our separate ways now, and pretend this never even happened."

"Well if that's how you feel, fucking forget it."

He now seems more annoyed than hurt. I suppose nobody likes being rejected, and being rejected by someone like me, under circumstances like this, must be particularly galling. He has offered the hand of friendship, only to have it swatted away by an ungrateful misanthrope. I can understand his rancour, but I still don't appreciate the slightly aggressive tone his voice has taken.

"Look, there's really no need for you to take that tone with me. I've tried to put it as nicely as I can. All I'm saying is that

48

neither of us stands to benefit anything from forging some sort of friendship with each other over a decade on from when we happened to be in the same maths class. And that's all we were, it's not like we were ever best mates or anything. I'm sorry if you're so desperate for friends that you would actually whore yourself in the street like this, but all I am trying to do is buy the paper and then go home. Is that too much to ask? To be able to perform a simple task without someone trying to crowbar their way into my life? I didn't set out today hoping to increase my circle of friends, and now that the opportunity has presented itself, I feel the need to do so even less. I don't want to be part of your life. I don't want to work in your bank. I don't want you to have my phone number. And believe me, you have nothing whatsoever to gain from being friends with me. I have nothing to offer you. *Nothing.*" Derek takes some time to absorb all I have said.

"Fuck you then you knobhead," is his considered response, and he turns and walks into the shop. Knobhead? How dare he insult me after wasting several minutes of my time? I storm purposefully towards the door of the shop, where I see him picking out a bottle of Lucozade from the fridge.

"Fuck you too you snotty-lipped twat," I yell at him. At last I can head home and read my paper in peace.

"Don't you *ever* get lonely though Gary?" Darren asks. Tonight Darren has left Aimee at home (either that or she has refused to return to my flat after the offence I caused her the other day. Perhaps that is another person I have permanently alienated) and he and Jimmy have come round for a few drinks, and after I've told them about what happened with Derek earlier today, the conversation has turned to my lack of relationships.

"I mean, people are meant to be with people," he continues, "it's just not the natural way of things for a human being to exist alone, without any sort of companionship."

"Well, maybe it's not natural for the likes of you." I pause for a moment to see whether either of them will react to "the likes of you", to see whether I provoke an outraged or offended response, but neither of them speaks up, and a wave of contempt towards them washes over me. "But it's natural for me Darren. It's not like I made a choice to think this way, it's just the way I

49

am, whether I want to be or not. I'm just not designed to be with other people, and I'm comfortable with that fact."

"That's just a bit weird though Gaz," says Jimmy.

"To you maybe, but to me, it's people like you that are weird; choosing to share practically every aspect of your life with another person, giving up all rights to privacy, unable to be on your own whenever you want, needing to get another person's blessing before you do anything; I can't understand that. And from what I've witnessed, people in relationships also become totally reliant on the person they're with. I've seen so many people change from being self-sufficient individuals before they enter into a relationship to complete wrecks who barely know who they are when that relationship ends. They just lose all identity. It's fucking pathetic. I have total autonomy over my life, and I am answerable to no one. Trust me, solitude and privacy are wonderful things, and they're not something I'd ever like to lose."

A few moments of silence follow. We continue drinking, and I can see Darren smiling to himself, and clearly mulling something over.

"What's on your mind Darren?" I ask him when he fails to reveal what it is.

"I was just thinking," he says, taking a swig of his beer before continuing, "how, if anyone was ever looking for a Lee Harvey Oswald style patsy, you'd be an ideal candidate."

"How so?" I ask, slightly offended, but also intrigued.

"Think about it. You're unemployed, you only have a few friends, you're a bit... unhinged, and you often express slightly inflammatory political views. Let's face it, if you were arrested for a political assassination tomorrow, I don't think any of us would really be *that* surprised. I can just imagine your Mum and Dad, neither of them wanting to believe it was true, but deep down there would be enough doubt in their minds for them to be convinced that it probably was."

"God yeah, you're right," says Jimmy, "and all your neighbours would be getting interviewed on telly, all saying things like 'oh he kept to himself really, he was a bit of a loner, always something strange about him'. All they'd have to do would be to plant some right wing literature and a few gun magazines in your flat and everyone would be convinced. It'd be

50

so easy. In fact, I think me and Darren should actually kill some high profile public figure and frame you for it, just to prove how easily it could be done."

I can't help but laugh at the whole concept. I don't think laughter was the reaction Darren was expecting his little theory to provoke.

"I find it a bit odd that you'd find that funny Gaz, I think most people would be pretty horrified to think that could apply to them."

"Well I'm not most people am I?"

"No, you're certainly not most people. The fact that you can't help but lace that response with a slight undercurrent of aggression being a case in point!" Darren's tone remains jovial, but I can see a seriousness sneaking into his expression. "You couldn't be much less like most other people. Doesn't that ever bother you?"

"What?" I ask. "The fact that I'm not exactly the same as every other fucking gobshite moron out there?"

"No of course not, but I can't help wondering how you're gonna feel in years to come?"

"About what?" I ask.

"In ten or twenty years' time, you might look back and regret not experiencing more of life while you had the chance. You've cut yourself off for so long, you don't get to experience the things that most people take for granted, and when you look back on your life, I worry that you're going to regret that."

"Well you needn't worry," I assure him, "I'm certain I'm not going to have any regrets. I think it's a complete fallacy when people say you regret the things you don't do rather than the things you do. I imagine that most people look back on their lives and regret almost every part of it. I think that, by having as little life experience as possible to look back on, one minimises the possibilities of having any regrets."

I suspect Darren and Jimmy are not entirely convinced by this. They probably believe I am merely insulating myself against regret later in life, or that I am reducing my chances of being "hurt". But they'd be wrong. I can honestly say that I believe my path to be the right one and that, ten or twenty years hence, if the three of us were to look back on our lives, they with a lifetime of broken relationships, shitty jobs, bad decisions and poor luck, and I with nothing but consistent mediocrity, I will be validated.

EIGHT

The next morning I wake up in the middle of one of the worst panic attacks I have ever experienced. The realisation that I have only a finite time before I have to find work has been ricocheting around my head since my last appointment with Brian, but it has now come to the forefront. My bed sheets are soaked through with sweat, and it's only the absence of pain in my left arm that convinces me I'm not having a heart attack. The only thing that can calm me down at a time like this is to clean my flat. And when I say clean my flat, I don't mean hoover and mop the floors and give the surfaces a quick wipe. I mean that every single corner of every single room needs to be cleaned thoroughly. When I do this, it will be done by a very precise system that I have perfected over the course of the last couple of years, and it will take me pretty much the entire day.

First I get out of bed and put my bed clothes, and any other clothes needing to be washed into the washing machine and put it on for an extra-long cycle with two additional rinses and an extended spin. I then put on a pair of tracksuit bottoms, T-shirt and socks which I keep in a polythene envelope in the top of my wardrobe and which I only wear on these days. Before I commence the job in hand I make myself a quick breakfast, as well as some sandwiches for lunch and some for tea. This way I minimise the amount of time I spend away from my cleaning, and also the amount of mess I will make later. Then I go to the cupboard under my sink and take out my cleaning items. In this cupboard I will, at any one time, have literally dozens of packets of anti-bacterial wipes, several pairs of rubber gloves and over a dozen bottles of bleach, cleaning sprays, oven cleaner, washing up liquid and even a couple of bottles of cleaning sprays that I have concocted myself. The mass of cleaning materials contained in this cupboard have become absolutely vital to me. Opening the doors and looking upon them fills me with the same awe a golfer might feel when looking at a pristine new set of clubs. I grab a handful of the wipes, put on a pair of rubber gloves and go back to my bedroom to begin.

First I wipe down every wall in the room, wiping in a vertical motion, top to bottom, followed by wiping along the skirting boards, starting nearest to the door and working towards the far corner. I then wipe down every surface in the room, wiping away from the wall towards myself. I hoover the parts of the carpet which are uncovered, then stand my bed up on its end and drag my chest of drawers into a corner that's already been hoovered before going over the rest of the floor. After wiping each door panel, starting with the top left panel and working in a clockwise motion, I repeat the whole process in the much smaller spare bedroom, and move onto the hallway.

Again I wipe the walls in the same manner described earlier. For the hallway skirting boards the method is slightly different. I begin at the furthest end of the hall, wiping along towards my bedroom, after which I hoover in the opposite direction.

The living room comes next, starting with another repetition of the wall and surface cleaning processes I have used in my bedroom. Then I move all my furniture (which consists of a three-seater couch, two single chairs and a small coffee table) from the wall they usually reside against, across to the opposite side of the room, allowing me easier access with the hoover. They are then moved back into place and the other side of the room is hoovered. After a short coffee and cigarette break I tackle the kitchen.

Firstly I take some flat cardboard boxes from on top of my kitchen cupboards, which I assemble and fill with all the contents of the cupboards and drawers. The cupboards are then cleaned one by one with a combination of the anti bacterial wipes and a bucket full of hot water, washing up liquid and a small amount of bleach. I also use some of my own recipe anti-bacterial spray (half a bottle of any decent anti-bacterial spray, topped up with lemon juice, bicarbonate of soda, salt and a squirt of bleach) on any parts of the cupboards or drawers which seem particularly unclean. Having finished this job and replaced the contents of the cupboards and drawers I move all my kitchen utensils, my kettle, toaster and microwave into one corner of the floor so I can thoroughly clean all the work surfaces as well as the cooker and hob. The floor is then thoroughly brushed and mopped and the kitchen bin emptied and bleached.

Moving onto the bathroom I take out a large can of bathroom mousse spray which, given that my bathroom is almost entirely tiled, is ideal for the task in hand. I generously spray the mousse over the toilet, sink, bath and floor and wall tiles. This mousse is most effective if left for approximately fifteen minutes so I take the opportunity to have another short food and cigarette break, after which I recommence in earnest. I use a separate mop to the one I use in the kitchen to mop the floor, then wipe down the toilet, bath and tiles in the same order in which I sprayed on the mousse. Particular attention is paid to underneath the lavatory rim, using a brillo-pad which I throw away as soon as it has been used. All this time I have been soaking an old toothbrush in a cup of bleach. I take it out and use it to clean in between every tile in the room, starting with the floor tiles nearest to the door, then moving on to the wall tiles, moving from the far wall, back towards the door. For the untiled parts of the room, a light spraying of one of the anti-bacterial sprays and a thorough wiping is sufficient. Finally, I pour about half a bottle of bleach into the toilet cistern, and flush the toilet ten times, before using the rest of the bottle on the toilet bowl. Having finished the bathroom, my flat is now clean. I take a slow walk through each room of the flat, minutely checking every single corner in case I have missed anything. I haven't missed a single spot. I never do. All that remains now is for me to clean myself. I put my cleaning uniform into my washing basket and get into the shower.

Usually when I have a shower, it's a thorough but relatively brief affair, normally lasting about ten minutes and having a comparatively simple system. On my cleaning days however, it's a different story. On these days I fill the bath to ankle level with very hot soapy water, and begin by shampooing my hair and work down my body towards my feet, using about half a bottle of shower gel. Using a bar of soap, I then begin again at my feet, this time working upwards and finishing with another shampoo of my hair. Switching back to the shower gel, I again work from my feet to my head. After rinsing this shampoo, and having switched again to the bar of soap, I wash myself down towards my feet. I empty the water out of the bath, and pour about a quarter of a bottle of shower gel onto each foot, then scrub both feet, starting at my left little toe, working towards my right big toe, then back again. The whole thing finishes with me rinsing my hair again and just standing under the shower for a good ten minutes. If, at any point during the shower, I feel that I have missed anything, or done something insufficiently, I will rinse myself off and begin the whole thing again. The whole process takes about forty minutes. By the time I've dried and dressed again, I have time merely to smoke a few cigarettes and drink a couple of beers and a glass of whiskey, after which it's just about time for bed. I know it won't last, but, for now at least, my mind is taken completely off my impending nightmare.

For me, this is a day well spent.

NINE

I'm not yet a total shut-in. I do still have a thin semblance of a social life, albeit one that consists of visiting my local pub once every couple of weeks or so with Darren and Jimmy. I don't do this for the social aspect, more for the fact that I enjoy draught Guinness. Although this is a regular occurrence and now part of my routines, I still find myself on edge beforehand. It is essential that I am not the first person there, which both Darren and Jimmy understand and indulge me in by ensuring that they are never late.

Tonight though, I initially find myself even more agitated than usual. As I order my first pint at the bar, my thoughts drift to my flat. I wonder whether I left everything where it should be before leaving. Did I make sure the door to every room was closed? Did I ensure my living room furniture was arranged correctly? How secure am I from burglars? What is the statistical likelihood of my building burning down in my absence? I carry my drink over to the table where Darren and Jimmy are sitting, a thousand troubling questions flying around my head. In my distracted frame of mind, I take a seat which places me with my back to the rest of the pub. I know as soon as I sit down that this is a mistake, as I always prefer to be facing a room. Halfway through my first pint I can feel my anxiety increasing, but am too embarrassed to request that either Danny or Jimmy, both of whom appear completely oblivious to my distress, swap places with me. In fact, they are contributing to my anxiety by allowing their conversation to drift, as it always does, to work. The office politics in Darren's workplace are a constant point of discussion, as is whatever computer software is currently being used to produce the magazine Jimmy works on. Usually these issues merely bore me, but tonight they are increasing my stress levels considerably. I feel myself constantly shifting in my seat, trying to catch a sideways glimpse of who is behind me. I feel that it is important that I get a full-on view of the rest of the pub in order to assess my situation so I make my way to the toilet, even though I could comfortably wait until the next round before I really need to piss.

The urinals are fairly crowded when I go in there so I waste no time in finishing. Upon turning towards the taps however, I am struck by a sudden feeling of dread about how many complete strangers must have touched these taps having just been handling their rancid dicks or wiping their arses. I begin to panic, but remember that I have brought a small packet of hand-wipes with me. I am acutely aware of how ridiculous I must look to anyone present as I take one wipe from my pocket to turn on the tap, then throw it into the bin before rinsing my hands, then take another one out to turn off the tap and yet another to switch on the hand dryer with. Despite this awkwardness, the reassurance of using them relaxes me enough for me to be able to take a slow walk back to my table, taking time to glance discreetly around the pub. I even have the presence of mind to turn my seat slightly to the side, giving me an acceptable side-on view of the pub. Sitting down, I feel a palpable wave of relief come over me and I am able to drop into the middle of the conversation. I even manage to stealthily steer the discussion away from their respective workplaces, without having to be particularly rude. Slowly the evening's earlier anxieties begin to dissipate and, with the help of some light breathing exercises and some more drinks, eventually they are all but forgotten and a couple of hours fly by in a swirl of cigarettes, decent conversation and pint after pint of Guinness, and I am relatively at ease. I haven't had an evening like this for quite some time. I'm actually finding moderate enjoyment being in company. I don't feel uneasy, I don't feel panicked.

"Christ", I begin to wonder to myself, "am I perhaps even on the verge of some sort of breakthrough here? Is it possible that I just needed one night of successful social interaction to act as some sort of a watershed and show that, just maybe, mixing with other people is not such a bad thing after all? If I can stand to be around people under these circumstances, maybe having to go to work could even turn out to be tolerable too? Could this simple evening in the pub with a couple of friends turn out to be the first steps on my very own Road to Damascus?"

Just before the anticipated call of last orders, I venture once more to the toilet. I approach the toilets infused with this new found positivity, so much so that as another patron sidles up to the urinal next to me, I even manage a half-hearted "Alright" to my fellow pisser. He nods in acknowledgement and we both face directly forward to answer the call of nature. Straight away though, something is not quite right. For a second, I struggle to place the source of my disconcertment, but, as I look down out of the corner of my eye, it becomes all too apparent. The man next to me is, inexplicably, pissing not in the normal way of pointing his dick down slightly, but is instead aiming it straight out at a 90 degree angle against the porcelain of the urinal. Inevitably, this is causing his piss to splash out in several different directions, such as directly onto my left hand and down onto my left trainer. At first I am too stunned even to comprehend what is happening and I stare in wide-eyed disbelief as the urine of this stranger continues to splash onto me. I suppose the common reaction in this situation would be for me to make some sort of protestation but I am so aghast I can't begin to form the words. As well as the many hygiene-related reasons for me to be upset, the first thing that springs to mind is simply "why me?" Why, out of all the people in this pub, out of all the piss-heads, the annoying old posh blokes, the loudmouth football fans, why did this man have to piss on *my* hand? On *my* jeans. On *my* fucking shoes. I also consider the possibility that this is no accident, that this is a deliberate act of urological aggression, directly designed to garner a reaction from me that would give him sufficient reason to kick my head in. It is quite possible that this man is a complete psychopath. Of course, it's also perfectly feasible that he has simply had a few too many drinks and genuinely doesn't realise what he's doing, and that bringing it to his attention will result in a swift resolution to my plight. But, I am now far beyond that. All I can do now is watch as my clothes, hand and shoes become soaked in another man's piss. Although urine is sterile while in the bladder, when it reaches the urethra it can become contaminated by surrounding tissue. Also, if this man has some kind of disease or infection of the urethra, I am at risk of infection, or at the very least a severe skin rash. The anxiety I felt earlier on in the evening has now come back with a vengeance. I finish pissing and, in my disquieted state I run out of the toilet, past my friends and without any sort of explanation I run home, throw my clothes and trainers straight into the washing machine and jump into the shower. It takes me the best part of an hour of vigorous scrubbing until I feel clean again. What a disastrous end to an evening that promised so much. I punch myself in the head over and over, furious that I could be idiotic enough to think that a couple of hours in the pub without a panic attack could be enough to offer any sort of hope for me.

TEN

Today is my dad's sixty-seventh birthday, and I have been invited round to my parents' house for a meal. This couldn't really have come at a worse time for me, but, after sustained pressure from Mum, I eventually accept. Unfortunately, Benjamin and his wife and child are invited too. Benjamin is the brother I have already mentioned. He is thirty-seven years old and couldn't be less like me. He is very wealthy, having opened up his own phone shop when he was in his twenties, just before the boom in mobile phones. This one shop was followed by several others as the demand and popularity of mobiles rocketed, until by the time he was thirty-two he was the owner of one of the most successful chains of independent phone shops in the country. His shops were eventually all bought by a major phone manufacturer, making him an instant multi-millionaire. He was also able to secure himself a highly paid position with the company who bought him out. He lives in a very exclusive and affluent part of Cheshire. I'm not even sure exactly where it is, but I can picture the kind of place; rows of houses with names instead of numbers, an attempt to give them a homely, English-country-cottage feel, when in fact the houses are surrounded by electronic gates, ten-foot high security walls and the most elaborate security systems money can buy. He lives there with his blonde trophy wife Annette and their five year old son Thomas. Like many people who've come from modest backgrounds to become wealthy, he carries with him a vague sense of embarrassment about his roots. Not that we've ever been working class by any means; I think it's the left-leaning and slightly hippyish inclinations of our parents that is the main source of embarrassment to him, as well as having a brother of whom he is truly ashamed. For as long as I can remember he has been an enthusiastic and outspoken Tory, with an admiration for Thatcher that sometimes borders on the sexual. As much as his political leanings are dictated by his wealth, they are I'm sure influenced by a desire to offend our parents and me. Benjamin and I have so little in common and converse so infrequently that Ben appears not to realise that I myself have no political allegiance at all, and therefore couldn't care less who he votes for. My brother and I have never seen eye to eye. There is less of a grey area as to whether or not I hate him. In fact, it's fair to say that I despise him, and that he despises me at least as much.

Ben and his family are already there when I arrive. Ben, Annette and I barely acknowledge each other as I hand my dad his present, one of those pretentious books that attempt to intellectualise football that he wanted.

"Oh, Gary. That's brilliant, it's exactly what I wanted. Thank you so much."

I can tell that my dad's gratitude is genuine. He puts his arms around me and gives me a big hug. I'm surprised when I register some semblance of guilt over the fact that I can't reciprocate. In the past I have tried faking it, making superficial attempts at this kind of casual affection, but it never convinced either me or the other person. My main concern now though, is that I feel very uncomfortable, and want to push my dad away from me. Thankfully, he lets go pretty quickly, no doubt remembering my issues surrounding physical contact. He walks into the kitchen where the rest of my family are gathered. I wander into the living room. A couple of framed photographs catch my eye on the bookshelf, and I walk over for a better look. In one frame, my brother, aged about six or seven, a thickly knotted school tie around his neck, grins happily; the kind of broad, toothy, unquestioningly happy grin children pull in school photos. Next to it is a photo of me, around the same age. I look as though I'm attempting to smile, but the look on my face is one of discomfort. Fear even. As school portraits go, it's a pretty poor one, and I wonder why my parents keep it. Then I realise, it is probably one of the few occasions when I have allowed anyone to take my picture.

My Mum eventually calls me into the dining room, and we all sit down to eat. I sit opposite Ben, with Thomas sat next to me. Although I don't particularly want to sit next to any of these people, I was especially hoping to be sat as far away from Thomas as possible. I don't like children. Children have no respect for boundaries. They have no adherence to the unwritten rules of the adult world. They will say what they want, when they want, regardless of how inappropriate it may be or how uncomfortable it might make someone. I know most people consider these things to be cutely innocent, but to me they are proof that children are simply not to be trusted. Especially over-privileged wretches like my nephew. As I take my seat I can feel the little brat staring at me.

"Why don't you ever smile?" he asks me.

"Thomas," Annette interrupts, "don't be rude."

I look down at him.

"Don't worry," I say, "one day you'll realise that there's very little in this world worth smiling about, and then you won't have to ask."

"Gary, don't be so mean," says my Mum, trying to disguise her anger. Dad looks disappointed with me. Ben and Annette look at me as though I have just punched their son, and the tone for the evening is set. Over the next hour I suffer through stilted and awkward conversation. My dad remains resolutely upbeat, Mum constantly looks at me as though preparing herself for me to say something weird or offensive, and I barely converse with my brother and his spouse. The worst thing of all though is that during this time the spoilt little sprog next to me has been constantly kicking me under the table. Not hard, just lightly, but enough to cause immense irritation. I ignore it as best I can. I may be an insensitive bastard but I have no desire to spoil my dad's birthday, and I know that I am incapable of either telling the child to stop or requesting that his parents do so without somehow causing a scene. The limits of my patience and self-control are reached and breached however, just as my mum is serving a fantastic looking homemade dessert. No sooner has the dish been placed on the table than Thomas kicks me as hard as he can in the shin. With this, I stand up suddenly, knocking my cutlery and glass onto the floor.

"Bastard! Fucking hideous little bastard," I scream at him. Everyone gasps in abject horror. Several admonishments overlap each other as Thomas bursts into tears and runs around to the other side of the table, where he buries his face in the surgically enhanced bosom of his mother.

"What the hell is wrong with you?" demands my brother.

"I'll tell you what's wrong with me, a fucking sore shin courtesy of Little Lord Cuntleroy over there. He's spent the entire evening kicking me under the table."

"Don't call my son a cunt! Why didn't you just say something? Either ask him to stop or tell us? For God's sake

63

Gary he's only five years old. He doesn't understand."

"Oh he understands. He knows exactly what he's doing. Besides which, it wouldn't be necessary for me to say anything if you hadn't spawned that little shit! Or if you'd at least raised your child NOT to kick people under tables."

"Don't call my son a little shit you fucking sociopath, and you are in no position to lecture me on anything," Ben says, standing up to face me, "least of all on how to raise a child. Once you've sorted your own sorry little life out, then you can begin to give people advice on theirs."

"It seems like you do need advice on how to raise a child, if that thing is the result of your parenting skills. In fact, I wouldn't be surprised if you put him up to it. It's probably your idea of fun you twisted fucker."

"I'm twisted? *I'm* twisted? You're the one who can't get through a day without dosing himself up on anti-psychotic drugs."

"You think you're so fucking superior, don't you Ben? You think you're so much better than me. You're not better than me; you're just a different type of cunt, that's all."

By now my Mum is in tears and my dad is just sitting there holding his head in his hands. I turn back to Ben.

"Jesus, this is probably the most we've said to each other in years," I say. Ben shakes his head.

"Go home you freak."

It takes me a full half hour to leave my parents' house. I had no wish to remain there, but I stayed anyway, just to piss my brother off a little more. I eventually leave the house, but not before nearly coming to blows with Benjamin after I had further insulted his wife and son.

When I get to the flat there is a van parked outside. Two men are unloading cardboard boxes and taking them round the back of the building. It appears I have a new neighbour to ignore. I slow my walk down as I reach the driveway, allowing the men time to disappear again so I can slip in my front door unnoticed. As I approach the steps to my door, the man at the back stops, places his box on the floor and begins to turn back towards the van, presumably having forgotten something. My only option now is to speed back up, and hope he hasn't seen me.

"Alright mate," I hear as I fumble in my pocket for my keys. I ignore him.

"Alright there mate," he says a little louder. There's no way I can pretend not to have heard him now, so I turn my head towards him. He looks about fifty, is fat with a big, untrimmed moustache. Faded green and blue tattoos cover the thick, trunk-like arms that protrude from his sleeveless T-shirt. I notice a thin, light, ring-shaped stripe on the ring finger of his left hand, indicating that he is recently divorced. This is the kind of person that ends up living in this building. Middle-aged divorcees like him, people recovering from some kind of addiction, and fuck-ups like me. But fuck-ups that usually leave each other alone.

"My name's John, I'm just moving in to flat 3," he says offering his hand for me to shake.

"Hello," I say, leaving his hand hanging.

"Erm... so we'll be neighbours then."

"It would appear so."

"So I'll be having a bit of a flat-warming this weekend, feel free to pop – "

"Listen John, I don't mean to be rude, but I really have to stop you there."

"Why's that?" John asks.

"Because you're new here, and obviously you don't really know how things work, and I don't want you getting the wrong idea about this building. Or the wrong idea about this flat anyway," I say, pointing upstairs to my flat. "See how it works is this; I don't really have much to do with anyone else here. I'm your neighbour only by virtue of the fact that we live in the same building. But I'm not someone who you can call on to borrow a cup of sugar, or ask to keep an eye on your flat while you're on holiday. And in return, I can guarantee that I will never bother you, never ask anything of you, and never disturb you. I've got nothing against you, John, and I hope that you will be happy in your new flat, and achieve whatever it is you want to achieve in life, but only if those things mean that we never need to converse. A passing 'hello' is fine, but no more than that. I can't speak for the people in the other flats, because I have the same arrangement with them. Maybe they're a bit more amenable, I really don't know. I speak only for myself, but I really hope you will respect my boundaries."

"Right. Ok. Yeah, whatever mate. You seem like a twat anyway, so fine by me."

"Thank you, John. I genuinely appreciate your understanding."

I'm glad he has decided to be reasonable about this, and I have not taken offence at being called a twat. I may have seemed harsh, but I think it is essential to establish such ground-rules as early as possible. We can now both go about our lives, free from unnecessary complications.

ELEVEN

The phone rings at exactly six o'clock. Nobody who knows me well would usually ring me at this time, because most people who know me are fully aware that from six o'clock until half-seven I am watching several different news programmes across the various channels. I probably watch more news programmes than anyone I know. Some people no doubt wonder why someone with such contempt for the world is so interested in the news stories developing in it, but those people misunderstand. It isn't the news itself that interests me, as much as the presentation. I find it fascinating to watch a report on any given news item on one channel, then to flick across to another network and watch their report on the same story. The reason I do this is to try and pick up on any subtle differences between the reports, the nuances of how the stories are put across to the viewers. On one channel, an innocent man dies as the result of police brutality and incompetence, on another channel brave police defending themselves from a deranged attacker are forced to shoot him. I suppose some people could watch the same two reports I have watched and find little if any difference between them, but to me, the differences are myriad and glaring. I find it incredible how cleverly and subtly viewers are manipulated by these reports, and fascinated by how easy it must be for the different news networks to push their own separate agendas. Which is why I am already less than happy when my phone rings. I am even less happy when I realise who it is that is making the call.

"Hello Gary, this is Ben."

"*Benjamin*," I say, sarcastically emphasising his name as I press the mute button on my TV, "just when I thought things couldn't possibly get any better, I receive a phone call from my favourite person."

I hear him exhale heavily at the other end. He's already vexed by my tone, a fact that brings me great satisfaction.

"Well, we haven't spoken since the... unpleasantness at Dad's birthday."

"No we haven't, but we've gone for much longer periods than this without speaking."

I look at the screen. A large building in a foreign country is engulfed in flames. People stand around in the street watching it burn. The shaky camera cuts between a woman screaming at the building, her tears leaving a clear trail through the thick layer of soot on her face, and an anxious looking reporter, his white shirt covered in debris and ash. I don't know where they are or what has happened, so I'm eager to get my brother off the phone so I can find out.

"That's true but, as you may or may not be aware, it's Thomas's birthday next week, and Annette and I would like it if you came to his party."

I haven't been invited to a single one of my nephew's birthday parties. And if I had been invited, I would most certainly not have attended.

"Why are you inviting me now? This wouldn't have anything to do with Mum would it?" I ask suspiciously.

"No," replies my brother unconvincingly, "we'd just really like it if you were there."

"I find that highly unlikely seeing as the last time we met I insulted both you and Annette and reduced Thomas to tears."

"Yes, I am well aware of that, but I'm willing to let bygones be bygones. We are brothers after all, so I think we should make some kind of effort to get along."

"Why?" I ask.

"Why what?"

"Why should we make an effort to get along? I mean, it's not like we ever have done before is it?"

"For fuck's sake Gary," Ben says, his own patience now evidently wearing thin with me, "I'm trying to bury the hatchet with you. Can't you just accept the fucking invite? Or if you don't want to accept it, just politely refuse it?"

"Look Ben, I know full well that you don't want me there, and you know full well that I'd rather die than be there, so why the fuck did you bother inviting me?"

"I only invited you because Mum practically begged me to. I have no desire to have you there, embarrassing me in front of my friends by acting weird, or upsetting the kids. I did this as a favour to her."

"Well do *me* a favour and shove your false invite up your arse, and tell Mum to stop interfering in my life."

"Tell her yourself you freak. And consider the invite well

and truly retracted," Ben yells.

"Oh boo-fucking-hoo." I begin to hang up, but stop just before I place the receiver down, and put it back to my mouth. "And don't ever ring me during the news again."

I slam the phone down, and settle back on my couch to watch the rest of the news. As I am about to turn the volume back up, though, something catches my eye, something unsettling. The chair in the far corner of the room is out of place. Not by much, in fact only by a fraction, but it's more than enough for me to notice. I rush over to the chair and move it slightly to the left, and stand back to look at it, but moving it seems to have made it worse. So I move it to the right. Still it doesn't look right. This time I try pushing it backwards, slightly closer to the wall. Now it looks completely out of place. "Shit, fucking hell," I mutter to myself as I pull it towards me. Now it looks totally alien. "Fucking cunting bastard fuck," I grunt, now just shoving the chair randomly around, no longer even sure what I'm trying to do. "FUCKING BASTARD!" I shout at the chair as I stand up and kick it as hard as I can.

"YOU FUCKING BASTARD PIECE OF SHIT CUNT!"

I run into the kitchen and grab the sharpest knife in there, then run back to the living room and slash wildly at the chair, stabbing and gouging at it until all its stuffing and spongy innards are hanging out. Grabbing the chair by its arms, I drag it through the front door of my flat and push it until it plunges noisily down the stairs.

I walk back into my living room, and see that the news has finished.

TWELVE

As with most British towns, violent street crime is common in Birkenhead. I know this because I have seen the statistics. I know this because I have read the newspaper reports and seen the local news programmes. And if I was ever in any doubt of this, then I have the point reinforced by that cunt Frank Field telling me that there was more violent crime in my hometown last year than there was in the entire country fifty years ago.

So I know this. And I know this despite never having been on the receiving end. I take measures to insulate myself against the possibility of falling victim to mugging and assaults. I do my best to stay away from certain areas of town. I rarely go out at night, and I don't own expensive items like an iPhone, iPod or iPad, and if I did I wouldn't display them in the careless way most people seem to.

These precautionary measures ensure that, as well as not having been a victim of street crime, I have never even witnessed it first-hand. Until today.

Grange Road West is hell at night, but in the day it is not much worse than any other town centre street, so I feel fairly comfortable walking down it. A few hundred yards ahead of me I see a man about my age walking towards me. He is engaged in the usual complacent texting, not looking where he is going, and completely unaware of his surroundings. If he had the slightest wherewithal, he would notice the man walking a few steps behind him. The man, wearing a tracksuit, a hoodie pulled up over his baseball cap for extra camouflage, couldn't look any more like a stereotype of the modern urban thief if he tried. He has probably been following this man for several minutes, just waiting for the most opportune moment to strike. Unfortunately for me, this moment comes when there is nobody but me in the vicinity.

Increasing his speed slightly, he draws up alongside his victim, grabs the phone with a practised hand, and sets off sprinting in my direction. The victim stares at his hand for a second, as though wondering whether his phone has simply vaporised, before looking up and seeing the thief running away, and beyond him, me.

"Oi! That's my phone, he's got my phone."

Great. Due purely to unfortunate timing, I am about to become directly involved in this piece of low-level street crime. The man is clearly shouting directly at me, there is nobody else on our side of the street, and is imploring me to act in some way. The mugger is now less than thirty yards away from me. I quickly run through my options;

1. I can simply ignore the mugger, and, not for the first time in my life, be thought a coward. If I take this choice, the only mitigation I could offer for my cowardice is that it is the man's own fault he was mugged, brandishing his phone in such a way. But this may lead to me being assaulted, as the man takes out his frustration on the nearest available person.

2. I could physically intervene, perhaps by tripping the mugger, or rugby tackling him to the ground, and risk being harmed by him.

Neither of these appeal, so I decide upon a third course of action. As the mugger reaches me, I reach my hands out as though trying to grab him, but make only the feeblest gesture of doing do, allowing him to knock me over without even breaking his stride. He turns the corner and he is gone. In my mind, I have struck the perfect balance. Without becoming too involved, I have now placed myself as another victim of this man's criminal acts, rather than the cowardly bystander I really am. His true victim doesn't seem to share my view. As he draws level to me, I expect him to help me up, but instead he looks down at me.

"What the fuck was that?"

"What? What do you mean?"

"That! You didn't even try to stop him. I only just bought that phone."

"Well that's not my fault," I say as I pick myself up off the pavement, "I'm not the one who robbed your phone. I tried to stop him."

"Oh yeah, you really tried your hardest there didn't you? You could have just tripped him up or something. Thanks a fucking lot mate."

He walks away from me, in the direction his assailant ran, and I am about to make a half-hearted defence of my actions, when I catch the eye of an old man on the other side of the street, who must have been watching as events unfolded. At first he looks empathetic, so I make a what-are-you-gonna-do gesture. Instead of reciprocating though, he just shakes his head in disgust and walks away. Behind him, the Hurst's Bakery window is full of faces, every single one of them laughing and pointing at me.

In the blink of an eye, I have become a public laughing-stock, and another one of Frank Field's fucking statistics.

THIRTEEN

The phone call I have been dreading comes as I am finishing off my third beer of the afternoon. A particularly smug-sounding employee of the Job Centre Plus rings to inform me that my first interview has been scheduled. It isn't for a specific job. The length of time I've spent on the dole means most employers wouldn't even consider me for an interview. Instead I've been sent to Workforce Recruitment. From what I can gather, they are a firm who interview people on behalf of actual employers, so they don't have to. It saves companies the time and effort of finding their own employees and, as part of any employees' hourly wage is paid to Workforce by way of recompense, it ensures that you actually get paid significantly less then you would if you had been recruited by the company itself. It seems that Workforce have placed themselves in an ideal position to profit from the desperate need that many people currently have to find work. No matter how dire things are for most people, there will always be some low-level fucker who can turn it to their advantage.

On the day of the interview, although it is not scheduled until midday, I've been up since half-seven preparing for it. It's not that I'm keen to be recruited or anything; rather that I am aware of what a delicate balancing act this will be. I am desperate not to be employed by this or any other company, but I know that the dole will contact any interviewers for a full debriefing on my performance. If it appears I am deliberately presenting myself as unemployable, I risk losing my benefits. It is therefore necessary for me to pitch myself just right. I must be dressed presentably, but not too impressively. I must appear keen, but not too keen. I would love to be able to go in and just act plain stupid, but I don't think I'm a good enough actor to pull that off.

I get to the recruitment office with only a few minutes to spare (I'm not late, so the dole can't penalise me for that if they do some snooping, and it might look bad in the eyes of the interviewer that I didn't get there earlier). Far from being the hub of activity, filled with energetic young go-getters that I had been expecting, the office is a pretty squalid-looking place, located above an Indian takeaway. The smell of fried onions and spices fills the stairway leading up to the agency. I enter through the main doors and approach the front desk, behind which sits a receptionist who looks like she should still be in school.

"Can I help you?" she asks without looking up from her computer screen.

"Yes, I have an interview with Mr Mitchell at twelve," I respond in a voice far more cheerful than my usual one. She still doesn't shift her glance from the screen. I wonder what she could be looking at on there that is so fascinating. Hardcore porn? Gruesome footage of road traffic accidents? Or perhaps there is nothing on the screen at all. Maybe the computer is actually switched off and this stupid little girl is merely staring at the dark glass of the monitor, watching her own vacant gaze staring back at her.

"Name?" she asks, as though this is all a huge inconvenience for her.

"Lennon, Gary," I reply, the initial chirpiness now drained from my voice.

"Sit over there," she says motioning with her head towards a row of chairs, "he'll be out in a minute."

"Thank you, you've been a tremendous help," I say sarcastically, but she doesn't even acknowledge me. I take a seat opposite her and watch as she picks up a phone and presumably dials Mr Mitchell, then replaces the phone, still without moving her eyes for a single second from that screen.

After about five minutes of waiting, a man walks through a door behind the front desk. I assume this is Mr Mitchell. He's a lot younger than I expected – about thirty – and is wearing a distinctly serious and unfriendly-looking expression. He leans over and says something to the receptionist who gestures towards me with a lazy sloping of her head, not moving the eyes that are still glued to the screen. Mitchell approaches me.

"Gary Lennon?" he asks. Before I can even answer he says, "Follow me," and leads me towards the door behind the front desk. As I pass the desk I arch my neck in an attempt to see what is on the screen, but the receptionist switches it off before I can see.

I follow him into an office which is bare other than two chairs on either side of a desk with a computer on it. On one wall is a large, framed print-out of a quote: "The man who does not work for the love of work but only for money is not likely to make money nor find much fun in life"; beneath which is a name I don't recognise. He directs me to a chair and takes his own seat on the opposite side of his desk. He picks up a sheet of paper which presumably is the curriculum vitae the dole faxed through on my behalf. It is probably the barest CV he has ever looked at. Mitchell throws the paper down onto his desk and leans back into his chair, his arms folded behind his head.

"So," he says, "what sort of work is it you're looking for?"

"I haven't really thought of anything specific to be honest," I reply clumsily.

"No, of course you haven't." I'm not sure what he means by this. He leans forward in his chair and places his hands flat on his desk. As he does this I notice the thick layer of dirt under several of his fingernails. They look like they haven't come into contact with a nail scrubber for weeks. The rest of him is fastidiously clean, and I am stunned that a man who is clearly very ordered could have missed so much filth. I am also hugely relieved that he didn't offer to shake my hand upon meeting me.

"Let me tell you the type of people we're looking for here at Workforce," he continues. "The type of people we want are hard working, conscientious, and reliable. We've got a very good reputation to maintain here. Companies know that when they recruit someone from Workforce, they're getting a good worker. Do you think you meet those basic criteria?"

"Well I like to think that I'm quite hard working, my time keeping is certainly above average and I'm pretty conscientious." I've pitched it just right. I sound keen and enthusiastic, but am giving myself a less than glowing tribute. Strangely, Mitchell pauses for several seconds and sighs heavily before responding.

"I've met you before," he says placing his pen down on his desk. I'm confused. It's pretty rare that I meet people at all, and I'm pretty certain I'd have remembered this one if we had indeed met, not least due to the hideous blackness under his fingernails.

"I don't think – "

"Not literally you," he interrupts, "but people like you. I've been in this game long enough to be able to spot your sort a mile off."

"I'm sorry, I'm not sure what you're talking about. What

does 'my sort' mean?" I ask nervously. He smirks smugly, and I almost retch as he briefly puts one of his filthy fingernails inside his mouth.

"It means the type of person who doesn't want to work, the type of person who takes the easy way out, who hides behind illness so they don't have to try to make it in the real world. The type of person who's probably never done a hard day's work in their life, instead relying on others for handouts and bleeding our economy dry. Have you got any idea how much hard working tax payers like me pay out to spongers like you every year? It's literally billions of pounds. *Billions*. Every single year. Just think of the good that could be done with that kind of money. Think what that money could do if it was ploughed into the school systems of the health service. People like you should be ashamed."

This is not what I was expecting. I thought this was going to be easy. I thought I could pull the wool over these people's eyes and go back to living my little life, at least until the next interview. But now I appear to have met my match. Still, all is not lost. Just because he's got my number, doesn't mean he actually wants to give me a job. He probably just wants to humiliate me a little then send me on my way, and if that's what it takes for me to get out of here with nothing having changed, then that's fine by me.

"I assure you Mr Mitchell, I—"

"If I had a pound for every time the dole sent me someone like you, I'd be able to retire to the Bahamas. I know exactly what you're trying to do. You're trying to look just interested enough to keep them from stopping your money, but not so interested that I actually give you a job. I've lost count of the number of times I've wasted my time interviewing someone like you, only to send them away without giving them a job."

Now this is what I want to hear, surely I'll be just another person to pass through his office and come out of it without having been forced to enter into gainful employment.

"But that's not what I'm going to do today."

Fuck.

"No, I've had my time taken up by wasters like you once too often. Today, Gary Lennon, you're going to leave this office with a job to go to. What do you think of that?"   He's on to me,

76

so there's no point keeping up the pretence any more. I want to point out the many inaccuracies in his little speech, to tell him what a hypocrite he is, castigating me for wasting tax payers' money, when he is making a living by exploiting those on the very bottom rung of the misery ladder. On any other day, I probably would do, but today, I just feel defeated. I loosen my tie and undo my top button.

"I think I should have got sent here a day earlier."

Mitchell turns to his computer.

"Now," he says, "I have absolutely no idea which job you'd be even remotely suited to, so I'm literally going to choose one completely at random for you."

He closes his eyes and pushes a key on his computer keyboard a few times. And with a few flicks of this man's slatternly finger, my life becomes a lottery. My mind fills with the possibilities of jobs that may come up. What jobs are out there? What do people actually work as these days?

"Perfect," he yells. "Park Communications Ltd. That's where you'll go. It's the call centre on Canning Street."

"A call centre? I have no idea what that is." I say.

"Well, have you ever had to phone a customer services line? To make a complaint or a general enquiry about something? About a product you've bought or a service you pay for?".

"No."

"Well, if you ever had, the place you would have been phoning is called a call centre. And the person you would have spoken to is called a Customer Service Advisor. And Customer Service Advisor is the job that you will undertake."

"That sounds... well, just fucking horrific," I say, my initial nerves and fear now giving way to anger.

"Believe me, it could have been a lot worse. I send people with far more going for them than you to much worse jobs than this. The other day I sent a man with a Masters degree to work in a biscuit factory. A fucking biscuit factory. And most of them are grateful to have a job to go to. This shouldn't be too taxing, even for someone with your limited capabilities. So long as you can switch on a computer, and form coherent sentences, even you should be able to manage." He prints off a piece of paper and slides it across his desk to me. "Be at this address at nine o'clock Wednesday morning. Goodbye Mr Lennon."

I take the paper and walk towards the door. As I'm halfway to it I pause and turn back.

"Just one thing."

"What?" Mitchell asks without looking up.

"Given all the advice and wisdom you've imparted to me today, I think I should in turn give you a small piece of advice."

He stops typing and looks up at me.

"What piece of advice could you possibly have to offer me?"

"Use some of that hard-earned money of yours to buy yourself a nail brush. Your fingers are fucking disgusting."

FOURTEEN

Tonight is the final night before I must begin work at Park Communications Ltd, and I intend to enjoy my last night of freedom. I initially consider inviting Darren, Aimee and Jimmy round to my flat for dinner and a few drinks, but, seeing as I'm about to be forced against my will to mix with people I realise that I'd much rather spend this evening in my own company, and decide to console myself by cooking my favourite meal. I walk up to Oxton village and treat myself to the thickest, juiciest-looking steak in the butcher's. I then buy a large bag of new potatoes and a selection of fresh vegetables from the greengrocer's. On my way home I stop off at the off-licence and buy the most expensive bottle of red wine I can afford. I take my catch back to the flat and begin cooking my indulgent dinner, accompanied by the sound of my favourite album, *Spiderland* by Slint, blasting out from my stereo. I begin by putting the potatoes on to boil while I slice up the carrots, peppers and courgettes, which I roast in the oven with some garlic and rosemary. Next I put some oil, salt and pepper into my frying pan and put it on the stove. When it's at optimum heat I throw in the steak. I take immense satisfaction from the huge sizzling sound the meat makes as it hits the pan, and I don't really mind too much when a few spurts of hot oil burn my forearm. I throw some chestnut mushrooms into the pan with the steak and watch them fry. By now the potatoes have boiled, so I drain the water off them. I remove the steak and mushrooms from the pan, and throw the potatoes in there with some garlic, salt and butter, and sauté them for a minute or so. I take the vegetables from the oven and put everything onto the plate, with a big fat dollop of blue cheese. I stand back and take a good look at the meal I have just prepared. I realise that while I may lack almost every other human urge and instinct – the urge to socialise, the urge to interact, the urge to fuck, the urge to love – I have still not lost the urge to eat. While almost every other thing which gives people pleasure may leave me cold, a good steak will never lose its appeal. Every animal under the sun must eat, and all of them enjoy fulfilling that urge. In that sense, and perhaps in that sense alone, I am just like every other living creature on this planet.

I take my plate through to my living room and sit down at the small table by the window. I pour myself a huge glass of wine and take a big gulp of it. I cut into my steak and watch the blood run from it and mix with the vegetables. Rare and bloody as hell, just the way I like it. For a moment I close my eyes, and imagine that I am a prisoner on death row. But my death will not be swift or humane. I am sentenced to the lingering, protracted death of working in a call centre. My execution is set for tomorrow morning, and this is the last meal of the condemned man.

FIFTEEN

I get to the office building a few minutes early. I stand on the other side of the road and have a last cigarette as I watch the droves of people entering through the glass double-doors. Plenty of them look almost as nervous as me, but I doubt very much that they are. In fact, I'm not nervous at all. I'm fucking terrified. I try to relax myself with a few breathing exercises, but it does no good. My hands are shaking slightly and I have a horrible feeling in my stomach. The same feeling I could read on the faces of those people on the train. Back then, I was a detached observer, but now am in the same sinking boat as them. I stub out my ciggie and walk across the road and through the main doors. I tell the security guard I am a new starter and am directed up to the second floor. On my way up I pass by the main room were I will be soon working. I stop and peer in through the glass panel in the door, to see row upon row of identical-looking desks. They seem to go on forever, stretching off into the far distance of the room. I listen to the constant chattering of people on calls, of phones ringing, of computer keyboards being furiously tapped, as it all melds into a horrible white noise, and feel as though I need to be sick. I continue up the stairs to a large conference room. I pop my head round the door to see several rows of chairs, in front of which there is a large presentation board. The seats are about half full and I walk in and take a seat at the end of the row that is least populated. Gradually more and more people file in. As the room fills I have the uncomfortable feeling that someone is staring at me. I turn my head to the row behind and a few seats to the left of me, and am surprised to find it is a very pretty girl, probably about my age. As our eyes meet she gives me a friendly smile. I quickly and embarrassedly turn to face back to the front of the room.

After a few more minutes an authoritative-looking man and woman enter the room and walk over to the board. Three people in red waistcoats follow them in robotically and sit in a row a few feet away from them. The woman takes a seat while the man steps forward.

"Good morning everyone," he says in a booming, confident voice. Most of the people in the chairs around me answer him as

81

though they were at a school assembly.

"My name is Mike Marsh. I'm the Project Manager and I'll be explaining a bit about what you'll be doing here at Park Communications Ltd. What we do here is provide outsourced call centre services for various companies. The company you'll be representing is a very well known catalogue, and it'll be your job to take orders, answer enquiries and deal with complaints from customers. Your campaign trainer will be Ruth Hughes..." He gestures towards the woman he entered with, and as he does so she stands, as though expecting a round of applause. With her voluminous hair, large breasts and excessive amount of make-up, she has the inexplicably tragic look of an ageing porn star. "...and these will be your Team Leaders." He gestures towards the waistcoats, who give half-hearted smiles. They all look like morons.

Mike launches into a long and agonisingly boring description of what our job will entail, and what it takes to do it successfully. I try to listen to him, but my mind begins to drift almost instantly, and it's not much longer before I feel my eyelids growing heavy. I pick up a few key phrases – mostly stuff about "service levels" and "teamwork" – before I eventually drift off to sleep. I awake with a jolt at the sound of someone sneezing behind me. I realise I've been asleep for nearly an hour and hope that I haven't been snoring.

"....and one last thing before we go to lunch." Mike turns over to a new sheet to reveal the word "ASSUME" written in large letters. "You should never assume because to assume makes an *ass* out of *u* and *me*."

To ensure everyone in the room understands this appalling play on words, he divides the word "'assume" up with strokes of his marker pen. With this a small but apparently genuine ripple of laughter passes around the room, and I almost want to cry.

We are told to take an hour for lunch and begin to file out of the door. God knows how I'm supposed to fill an entire hour. A few people seem to have formed instant friendships and wander off towards the main exit, presumably heading to the pub or the café around the corner. Most of us, though, head towards the canteen. I get myself a coffee from the machine and take a seat on my own in the far corner. A large bunch of people stand at the other end of the room, all making small talk. The seat I have taken faces towards this group, and my mind starts to drift as I watch them. When I finally snap out of my day dream I realise I am looking at the pretty girl who smiled at me earlier. She gives me another friendly smile and I quickly turn my head away and look out of the window. Out of the corner of my eye I am horrified to see that she is now walking towards me. I keep my gaze fixed firmly on the window as she reaches my table.

"Hiya," she says after a slight pause. I look up at her.

"Erm... hi," I reply nervously.

"Mind if I sit down?" she asks, already pulling a chair out for herself.

"Erm... no, go ahead."

"I'm Jenny." I feel very relieved that she doesn't extend her hand for me to shake. The way I feel today I would definitely need the reassurance of a hand-wipe if I made contact with anyone.

"Gary," I reply.

"What do you reckon so far then?"

"About what?"

"About this place. About Mike and Ruth, and the job and everything?"

"Well from what I've seen of the place so far, it's kind of like a hospital. All the team leaders are like the doctors, but instead of monitoring heart rates and blood pressure, they've got those computer screens where they monitor the length of the calls, the length of everyone's lunch breaks, and the amount of time it takes someone to have a shit. The workers are like the patients, except that instead of life machines, they're all attached to those phone headset things we'll soon be wearing. I've been wondering whether they'd start gasping for breath and needing resuscitation if their phones were detached from them. Mike looks like Val Kilmer's boring younger brother and talks like a robot that's been programmed with a mildly charismatic personality. Ruth looks as though she's spent the last twenty years of her life getting fucked on camera, and it's finally started to take its toll. As for the job itself, I think the best I could possibly hope for is that it pays my way while it corrodes my soul."

"Ha ha ha, nice one!"

Jesus, she actually thinks I'm funny. I'm a bit confused. It's usually at this point that most people would simply walk away from me. My impromptu little rants have a habit of sending people scarpering, but this one is actually laughing.

"Yeah, I know what you mean. Bit fucking depressing isn't it? It's all bollocks really but we've all gotta pay the bills and this job's as good as any other I suppose."

I'm not sure if I'm expected to respond to this, and have nothing much to say, so instead I nod my head a little before Jenny carries on talking.

"I mean, I've just got back from travelling the Far East for nine months, so the last thing I want to be doing is sitting behind a desk answering phones, but what are you gonna do?"

I detect that this time I am expected to contribute to the conversation. I've been asked a direct question, of sorts, so I have to formulate a response.

"I suppose it beats resorting to street muggings or prostitution," is the most civil thing I can come up with. I'm amazed to see a comment that would normally engender offence greeted with yet more laughter.

"Yeah I suppose it's just preferable to those things. And you never know, it might just be a way to meet interesting new people."

For this I certainly have no reply. There is a pause during which Jenny looks me straight in the eye. I have to look away after a few seconds. After what seems like a very long time she stands up.

"Well I'm gonna get a coffee and eat my lunch before we go back in. It was nice meeting you Gary."

"Yeah. Erm... you too."

And she walks back to the group of people she came from. I take my coffee outside and light up a cigarette. So far, this place is even worse than I thought it would be. As I smoke I consider simply walking home and never returning, but something stops me. If I did just disappear, I will be unemployed and without my benefits. For this reason alone, I have to force myself to go back inside.

After lunch we are divided up into three groups and herded like concentration camp detainees through three separate doors.

My group, which includes Jenny, is taken into a smaller conference room where we are greeted by one of the waistcoats from earlier on. He motions for us all to sit down.

"Hi, my name's Richard, and I'll be your team leader while you're working on this particular campaign," he announces pompously. "I've been working here for five years now. I started off just where you all are, but I worked hard and worked my way up until I got to where I am now."

Apparently, being a team leader in a shitty little call centre is reaching some sort of zenith, and he clearly thinks we should all be impressed by his life's trajectory, and be honoured that such a man of influence is granting us an audience. I quickly come to the conclusion that Richard is an ugly, acne-scarred little cretin.

"You'll find me firm but fair", he continues, seemingly trying to use as many clichés as he can in as short a space of time as possible, "if you do right by me, I'll do right by you."

By now my head is beginning to ache from the onslaught of this man's multiple platitudes. My poor concentration span has kicked in and my eyes wander around the room. I count the number of windows in the room (8), the number of carpet tiles between me and the door (426) and the number of air conditioning vents (4). Eventually my eyes drift to the row of chairs in front of me. My eyes move along the line looking at the backs of people's heads, and I wonder if I can guess what they look like. After guessing that one grey-haired man looks a bit like Oliver Reed, I am surprised that the next head is facing towards me and belongs to Jenny. She motions towards Richard, who I've long since managed to block out, and makes the universal "wanker" sign with her hand. I involuntarily let out a loud laugh and seemingly the entire room turns to look at me. I look up at Richard and he too is staring at me, with a face like thunder.

"Is there something funny?" he asks.

"I'm sorry?"

"I said is there something amusing that you'd like to share with us?"

I object immensely to the condescending tone in which I'm being spoken to, and I search for a quick and witty rejoinder. A few spring to mind; *"The only thing I would ever like to share with you would be a deadly disease you ugly little fucker"* or *"yes, I would like to share with everyone present that I consider you to be a contemptible, vile little shit"*. I wonder what Oscar Wilde would say in this situation, but then realise the chances of Wilde ever having had to take a job as degrading as this are slim.

"Erm... no, nothing. Sorry," I mumble pathetically.

Richard walks away and continues his team-talk, satisfied that he's used me to assert his alpha-male status, and I feel completely humiliated. I can see Richard and I are not going to get along.

SIXTEEN

The following morning I report, per my instructions, to the training room on the ground floor of the building. The room is full of exact replicas of the work stations we'll be sitting at when our training is over. I'm one of the first people there and I take the desk farthest from the door. I do a few of my breathing exercises to try and relax myself. The rest of my team gradually start to file in and I try to avoid making eye contact with any of them in case they mistake it as a friendly gesture and sit next to me. There is one person, however, who clearly doesn't need an invitation, as Jenny soon sits down right beside me.

"Morning," she says in a voice that's far too cheerful for this time of day.

"Hello," I reply in a voice far more befitting the circumstances.

"Fucking hell, you really sound like you need one of these," she says, placing a huge cappuccino on the table next to me.

"Wow, thanks," I say, choosing not to mention that I usually wouldn't dream of drinking the kind of ostentatious, foaming coffee that is peddled by the many multinational chains this country is now full of. Coffee used to be a simple drink people used to get themselves through the day. You could have it black, or with milk. That was it. Now it has taken on a bizarre, fetishistic status. It's not just a drink anymore, it's something people base their social lives around, it's a status symbol. Nobody is anybody now unless they have a massive cardboard cup full of frothy coffee.

"What's this for?"

"Well I wanted to apologise for getting you into trouble with that tool Richard yesterday. If I hadn't have made you laugh it never would have happened."

"No, it's OK, you weren't to know I'd laugh like a fucking fog-horn. Plus it's probably my own fault for allowing myself to be talked down to by someone who looks like an officious meerkat. With acne."

Our conversation is cut short by the arrival of Ruth the trainer. As much as I'm dreading the monotony of learning to do this job, I'm also relieved that I don't have to continue making small talk. Jenny seems like a nice enough girl, but I've been out of the social loop for a long time, and there's only so much conversation I can take at once, so I find the mind-numbing directions of Ruth quite a welcome distraction.

We are told to open the drawers of our desks and take out our instruction manuals, which Ruth ludicrously refers to as our "Bibles". According to her, these will tell us absolutely everything we could wish to know about our job, which makes me wonder why on earth they bother to employ her. Regardless, she sets us to work. The manuals guide us through several examples of the typical types of phone calls we will receive in an average day here. There are then several exercises for us to do, to give an idea of how we will deal with the calls on the computers. For the most part they are very easy, and anyone with a rudimentary knowledge of computers should be able to navigate them fairly simply. I am about halfway through the exercises when Jenny leans across to me.

"What do you do after you've put the customer's payment details in on the order page?" she asks. I suspect she already knows the answer to this question and is just using this as an excuse to talk to me. As I am about to lean over and demonstrate on Jenny's keyboard, Ruth suddenly appears between us and blocks my path.

"It's Gary isn't it?"

"Yes it is."

"How are you getting on?"

"Erm yeah, fine I think. No problem."

"Let's have a look at where you're up to."

And with that she puts her hand on my shoulder and bends over, ostensibly for a closer look at my computer screen. However, I wonder if it is merely a coincidence that her stance gives me a clear view down her top to her breasts, which are approximately five inches from my face.

"Yes you seem to be getting on fine," she says, standing back up again, but leaving her hand on my shoulder. Her hand lingers for what is probably a few seconds but seems like aeons to me. I feel the urge to pick up the ruler from my desk and swat her hand away like a fly.

"If you need any help with anything Gary, just let me know."

Her hand slides down my arm in what I'm sure is meant to be a sensual and seductive manner. The only effect is has on me, however, is to make me feel slightly nauseous.

"Oh my fucking GOD!" Jenny says as Ruth finally walks away. "One of the bosses just made a pass at you!"

"Oh I'm sure she didn't. She was probably just being friendly or trying to help or something," I say, knowing full well that Jenny is right.

"Come off it Gary, the dirty old slag wagon was properly flirting with you!"

"Yeah I suppose she was," I admit.

"There's no suppose about it!" She's laughing, but I detect just a tiny hint of resentment in Jenny's voice, which makes me feel very uncomfortable. What the fuck is going on here? How did this happen? In the space of a few days, I appear to have been unwillingly transformed into some kind of call-centre Don Juan, with women who could frankly do much better apparently ready to come to blows to win my affections. If only they realised that I have no affection to give. At times like this, I wish I was hideously ugly, or at least just plain. Plain people have the ability to become invisible. I'm not saying I'm stunningly handsome, but someone like me is just slightly too good-looking to be able to truly disappear into the background, avoiding situations like this.

"Excuse me," I say, and go to the toilets and lock myself in a cubicle. By now I'm almost hyperventilating. I feel like one of those kids who have no natural immunity against germs or infections, and have to live most of their lives in some sort of tank or bubble. I have had my bubble ripped from me, and have no protection against this much human interaction.

When I get home I lock the door. Today is April 17th, my birthday. I am now 29 years old. This fact is of absolutely no consequence to me. I have never understood the fuss about birthdays, the way people need to mark them. What exactly is it that they are celebrating anyway? The fact that they've managed to survive yet another year without giving in to the urge to blow their fucking brains out? It's just the passing of another 365 days, so what the fuck is there to actually celebrate? All it means is that we are another year closer to death. Then again, maybe that's

89

what people are actually celebrating. Personally, I haven't actively celebrated a birthday since I was ten, and even before that, I think I only had birthday parties because my parents took it on themselves to arrange them for me. Now I have the right not to celebrate at all, and it's a right I take full advantage of. For the rest of the day I will not leave the flat for a single second. My family and friends have chosen not to respect my choice, and insist on sending me cards and phoning me to wish me a happy birthday, so I unplug my phone, switch off my mobile, refuse to answer my door and anything in my mail which even vaguely resembles a birthday card will be thrown straight into the bin. I spend the rest of the day reading, watching television and eating. At about half-ten I put on my DVD of *Network*. Round about the time of Ned Beatty's rant to Peter Finch about Arabs buying America, the clock turns midnight. Another birthday has been and gone. Big fucking deal.

SEVENTEEN

For the next few days I do my best to keep my head down and get to the end of each shift with as little awkwardness and contact as possible. Unfortunately it is impossible to remain completely anonymous when forced into the company of others. And the harder you try to become invisible, the more people will notice you. Towards the end of my first full week I'm standing outside having a cigarette, looking into the car park to the side of the building. There are hundreds of cars in there, and even from where I'm standing I can see at least a dozen people sitting in their vehicles, eating their lunch. This strikes me as a truly bizarre phenomenon. Of course, I can relate to their desire to be left alone and not mingle with the people inside, but even I would not go to such extraordinary lengths. I prefer the simpler methods of burying my head in a book or newspaper while on my lunch break, or just not staying in the same place for too long. If you stay in the same seat for more than ten or fifteen minutes, the likelihood is that someone will attempt to talk to you. It's important to break it up by going outside for a smoke. But doing something as obviously evasive as sitting in your car to eat your sandwiches just makes you look pathetic. I can't tell from here, but I imagine they all have their car stereos turned up as loud as they will go to drown out the sound of their own sobbing.

Out of the corner of my eye I see a small group of lads coming out of another door about fifty yards away. I recognise them as all being in my team, but have never spoken to any of them. They are chatting away to each other when I hear a shared outburst of laughter. As there is only me and them in the vicinity, I naturally assume that their laughter is directed at me. I start to panic a little. My breathing quickens instantly and I feel a layer of sweat forming on my back. Fuck, I've been here only a few days and people are already laughing at me. I knew they'd discover what a weirdo I am eventually, but I didn't expect to be found out as early on as this. I thought perhaps I would humiliate myself a few times, and gradually alienate my co-workers with inappropriate remarks and a refusal to laugh at their jokes. But it appears I don't even need to do that anymore. I can do all that simply by existing.

"Oi mate!" I hear one of them shout. Christ, what now? Not content with making jokes at my expense amongst themselves, do they now intend to openly mock me? I ignore the shout.

"Eh, lad!" The same one shouts again. What am I supposed to do? Turn and defiantly stick two fingers up at them? Pull down my trousers and moon at them? Again I decide simply to ignore him. This does nothing to deter him, and he now begins to approach me. Am I about to be assaulted by this man? What is my best course of action here? Do I wait for him to get within striking distance and launch a surprise attack? Or should I simply turn and run? In my indecision I do neither, and he is now right next to me.

"Alright mate, how's it going?" I'm surprised by the friendly salutation.

"Erm, fine thanks."

"You're on our team aren't you? Do you wanna come and join us?" he asks motioning towards the rest of the group. Naturally, I want to say no, but I find myself following him back to his friends.

"I'm Dave, this is Steve, Mark and Lee," he says, introducing the whole group. To my horror each of them has extended their hands for me to shake. My mind races as I try to conjure up a way to avoid shaking their hands, but I come up with nothing.

"I'm Gary," I say, reluctantly giving each of them the kind of limp handshake that usually results in suspicion and mistrust. I reach inside my pocket, planning to discreetly make use of a hand-wipe. It's only then that I realise I have left them all in my bag upstairs.

"We were all just talking about that Ruth one," I hear someone say.

"What about her?" I ask with my mind focussed solely on the fact that I need to wipe my hands.

"We were just discussing," says Lee, "whether or not we'd fuck her."

"I definitely would, she looks like a right fucking dirty bitch," Dave says, thrusting his pelvis rhythmically at thin air.

"Yeah definitely," agrees Mark lasciviously, "I know she's a bit old but I reckon she fucking loves it up her. And coz she's getting on a bit so she's probably a bit more desperate so she'd let you do pretty much anything to her."

"What about you Gary?" Steve asks the question I've been dreading.

"No," is my flat response. A pause ensues where I am no doubt expecting to spell out my reasons in the crudest language possible.

"Why not?" Dave asks when I'm clearly not going to be any more forthcoming. How am I supposed to answer this question? Am I supposed to tell them that I wouldn't fuck her because the thought of having sex with anyone makes me feel physically sick? Or that it's been so long since I had sex that, even if I wanted to, there's a good chance that I'd have forgotten how to do it? Or should I tell them that the thought of sex with Ruth, or with anyone for that matter, is far less a priority than the fact that I am desperate to remove the dead skin cells and dirt that they have all passed onto my hand?

"She's just... not my type," I say eventually, hoping that they will get the hint and either shut the fuck up and let me go or at least change the subject.

"Bet you wouldn't say that about that Jenny though would you?" Dave persists.

"What's that supposed to mean?"

"Nothing, it's just that it's obvious to everyone that she's got a bit of a thing for you."

"Yeah," says Steve, "you lucky bastard, she's well fit."

"And that Ruth looks like she wouldn't mind a bit off you too." I'm not even sure who is talking now, the need to wipe my hands now my sole focus. "You should get them into a threesome, fucking fling it right up the pair of them."

"Fling it up them"? Christ, is this really how men are supposed to talk? Is this what passes for male banter?

That's exactly what I'll do," I want to yell in their faces, *"I'll get the pair of them, and fucking use them like worthless whores .I'll fucking spit on their faces and slap them into submission. I'll fuck their arse holes until they gush with blood. I'll make them both gag on my cock until they fucking asphyxiate. I'll make them lick my arse hole and fist them both until their cunts rip apart. I'll piss all over them and make them shit in each other's mouths. Then I'll jizz in their eyes so much they both go fucking blind. I'll do it, because I'm a fucking man, and because it's what you lot, my fellow men, my supposed fucking peers, expect of me, and I'm so fucking desperate for your fucking approval and acceptance that I'll happily do all of these things, and much worse besides, in order to gain it. Are you fucking happy now? Is that what you want to hear you fucking bunch of animals?"*

"I'm going back up, I'll see you all back up there."

I turn and walk quickly through the door. I hear one of the lads say something to me but I'm not listening. I walk as fast as I can back to my desk and grab a hand-wipe out of my bag. I head into the toilet to wipe my hands with it. The relief this brings is immeasurable. I wish I could stand here at the sink wiping my hands for the rest of the day. The thought of any more of these moronic conversations fills me with dread.

After wiping my hands, I walk back into the canteen, where I take a seat with Jenny and a few others, who are all making the usual getting-to-know-you small talk. I'm fascinated by the ease with which the conversation flows between the rest of the group. Conversing with groups of more than one or two other people is something I've always had immense difficulty with, but these people are all adept at it. I wonder whether, if I hadn't withdrawn so much over the years, this is a skill I too would have developed. I conclude though, that some people are just naturally at ease with others, and that there are some, like me, who simply don't belong amongst other people. As these people sit here discussing their lives and sharing their opinions and experiences, I realise that there is one advantage I have over these people; because I've been disconnected for so long, I am now a blank canvass. Through all the people they've met over the course of their existence, the lives of these people have tentacles that extend far beyond this room. If they lie about their past, there are hundreds of other people who can expose their lies. But because my entire circle of friends and family is less than ten people, I could, should I so wish, create an entire new history for myself. I could tell them I've been working as a missionary in South America for five years. I could tell them I'm an eccentric rich philanthropist, a serial killer, a former Jesuit priest, a respected painter, anything I want. I have the ability to create an entire new persona for

94

myself, and the chances of my lies being exposed are slim, because there are so few people to verify or deny them. Of course, I don't have a sufficient desire to impress any of these people to actually want to do this, but I'm fascinated by the potential to create a whole new Gary Lennon.

After a few minutes, this group conversation turns to current affairs, or to be more specific, the headline on the front page of somebody's copy of *The Sun* newspaper. The headline article in question concerns the conviction of a paedophile who had abused several children over a course of many years. This is exactly the kind of conversation where my views are likely to differ from the average person, so I quickly make the decision not to become involved. The usual, predictable, ill-informed comments abound. "String the lot of them up I say," offers one person. "Fucking animals, they should castrate them all," says another. Every person present seems to be contributing some such unoriginal sentiment, with the exception of Jenny, who has timed a visit to the toilet well enough to avoid it, and myself. "Please don't let them ask for my opinion", I think to myself. It seems someone is reading my thoughts though, and doesn't want to let me off the hook that easily.

"What do you think Gary? They're all fucking evil aren't they?" I'm not even sure who has asked the question, but everyone is looking at me, waiting for my response.

"Well I suppose it depends what you mean by evil," is an answer they clearly weren't expecting.

"What do you mean by that?" someone asks.

"Well," I continue, "if by evil you mean that they commit sinful or wicked acts, then yes, they probably are, but what you're failing to consider is what drives them to commit such acts. I mean, are these people inherently evil? Are they born with a desire to cause suffering and inflict harm upon others? Or is there some reason why they become the way they are? Have they themselves been abused in some way, which makes them perpetuate this cycle of abuse?"

"Oh don't tell me," says one middle-aged Dennis Franz look-alike I haven't actually met until now, "you're one of those liberals who thinks that paedos are all victims who somehow deserve our sympathy, and should be treated in hospitals or some shit instead of being put in prison for the rest of their lives where they belong, so they can't harm more innocent kids?"

I can't help but laugh at him.

"What the fuck are you laughing at? You think kids being abused is funny?"

"Of course I fucking don't. I just find people who clearly have no perspective on a subject expressing their views so vociferously amusing. And only somebody as clueless as you could ever think of me as a fucking liberal. Frankly I couldn't care less whether paedophiles were all gassed or whether they were taken into some sort of Clockwork Orange type programme where the desire to re-offend was scientifically removed. It couldn't possibly make any less difference to me. I'm just answering the question that someone asked me, so don't get upset by the fact that I don't agree with you all. Also, I find the fact that you are reading about this particular case in *The Sun*, a newspaper which reports these matters in such an exploitative, sensationalist way, hypocritical in the extreme. They report in such a way in order to whip all their readers into such an indignant frenzy that they get swept along by the headlines, without looking into the deeper sociological factors or any possible mitigating circumstances, just so that they can sell more newspapers. Did you know that incarcerated paedophiles actually consider newspaper reports like that to be the closest thing they can get to child-porn? I mean, they actually masturbate to them! So don't think for a second that *The Sun* or any of those other papers actually care about the children this man abused. All they're doing is exploiting things like child abuse cases for their own gain, and that doesn't do anything to help the actual victims of these crimes. All it does is give people like you something else to take the moral high-ground over, without knowing the first fucking thing about it. Also, I resent the way in which you asked me that question. You clearly assumed I shared your opinion on the matter. Please don't ever assume I share your viewpoint on anything, because in all likelihood, I don't share your views on one single issue. And like Mike says – 'to assume makes an *ass* out of *you* and *me*'."

The assembled group look at each other, some shaking their heads, some dumbfounded by what I've said, and I remember being 14, standing at my grandmother's death bed. She had been dying for years. I had no memory of her being young, fit or

96

healthy, so when she died, it seemed to me like the inevitable conclusion. My extended family were in tears, hugging and consoling each other, but I was unable to cry. The disapproving looks my family gave me on that day were the same as the stares I am now receiving from my co-workers.

"I don't think any of us would want to share the kinds of views you have, lad," says Dennis Franz.

And with that, one by one everyone simply gets up and leaves the room. This, rather than that of Jenny, is the kind of reaction I am more accustomed to. Within seconds I am left alone, just me and the bland austerity of the canteen. Not for the first time in my life, I have managed to alienate a large group of people simply by opening my mouth. Far from feeling rejected, I take a certain comfort in the solitude I am now afforded. At least I won't have to listen to the hypocritical, ignorant views of others.

EIGHTEEN

From the window of my second bedroom, I have a clear view of the car park at a local lower league football stadium. On the penultimate Sunday of every month they host a car boot sale. This is a phenomenon which has never failed to grab my attention. Each time it occurs, I get up early to watch the cars roll in one by one and, using my binoculars, I witness the events unfold. I sit by my window with some coffee and toast and watch with morbid fascination as swarm upon swarm of people, some of whom actually drive many miles to come here, scramble around each other, each trying to beat the other to the cheapest pile of unwanted records or bag of old clothes. I observe with a mixture of horror and amusement as they haggle and barter over the price of a box of CDs without even bothering to check the contents. I see a middle aged couple share a look of triumph as the spending of £2 secures them a tattered old chair, which one can imagine having languished in a spare room after being used by somebody's now deceased grandmother. Every time this thing occurs I see the same callow, blank faces turning up here to scavenge and forage. What brings these people here?

After the 1950s, the ship-building industry that employed tens of thousands in Birkenhead was in steep decline, and in the 80s, unemployment here rocketed. Thatcher's Britain meant towns like this were basically left to rot. With the town crumbling, few prospects and a heroin epidemic taking hold, things were very fucking bleak indeed. Many people, in desperation, even began frequenting the local tip, sorting through endless piles of refuse in an attempt to find something, anything they could use or sell; "tipping" they called it. Some people even went so far as to find food there. Birkenhead, despite a few attempts at regeneration, has never truly recovered from that time, and to me, these car boot sales seem like an extension of the tipping, legitimised only by the exchange of small amounts of money.

All frequenters of this ugly farce appear to enjoy every minute of it. They arrive with smiles on their faces, and as they leave their smiles have only broadened, save for the disappointed few who leave empty handed.

I have in the past considered the possibility that I may be the one who is wrong, that the distaste I feel for such things is merely another indication of how out of touch I am. Maybe there is nothing wrong with these people finding pleasure in things which bemuse or repulse me. I turn my binoculars away from the car boot sale and lift them towards the sky. The dark Birkenhead sky, one unending collage of many shades of grey. Sitting here, under these skies, above these people, I truly do feel like the last sane man on earth.

NINETEEN

"So I'll call you in a minute from my desk, and you just answer it as though it's a normal call. I'll ask a few normal questions about a few products, them eventually place an order. You just answer the way you normally would if it was a customer calling."

I have just signed on for my shift, and Steve from Quality Control is trying to gain my cooperation, but I really can't see his point.

"What, even though I know full well it's you?"

"Yes. It's not that complicated."

"I know it's not complicated, it's just preposterous."

"It's not preposterous; it's just something we need to do on a weekly basis. We need to know you are fully conversant with all the scripts, all the product details, and that your customer interaction is as good as it can be."

"Despite the fact that you can gauge all those things by listening in to our calls, which you do on a *daily* basis?"

"Yes Gary," Steve is rubbing his eyes now, "despite that."

"Well, as I said, it's preposterous. A complete waste of time."

"Look Gary, this is just something that needs to be done. It has always been done. We've done it since this place opened. We still do it now, and we will do it for a long time after you leave. I don't know why, but it's something we do."

"And you just go obediently along with it, no matter how pointless it is? Just because it has always been done? Presumably if the company told you that all Quality Control officers were required to insert broken glass into their anus each morning, you would unquestioningly do that too? Fine, do what you must, but get it over with for God's sake."

Steve walks back to his desk and calls my phone direct. I let it ring for a full half minute before I answer.

"Hello."

"Yes, I'm thinking of placing an order, but I have a few questions about some of your items that I'd like to ask first."

I let a long silence hang between us. Of course, Steve is the first to break it.

"Hello?"

"What are your questions?"

"Gary... I thought we had agreed you'd treat this like a normal call? You're not even being civil, never mind providing excellent customer service."

"I never agreed to treat it like a normal call. I said do what you must. If you find it absolutely necessary to take part in this ridiculous charade, that's fine, but don't expect me to go along with it."

"Jesus Christ, just forget it, I'll ask someone else."

Steve finally gives up and slams the phone down. I take the opportunity to remove the bottle of anti-bacterial spray from my bag and spray it liberally over the computer keyboard. I then take out my hand-wipes and carefully wipe the keyboard down, being sure to get right in between all the keys. I put the mouse mat in a drawer and take my own from my bag, placing it under the mouse. Recent studies have shown that the average office work station contains more germs than a toilet seat. It's galling enough to have to breathe the same air as these imbeciles, there's no way I'm prepared to catch any of the germs they are no doubt riddled with. As I place the spray and wipes back into my bag, I notice Jenny sitting a few rows away. She is at her desk, and one of the other lads in the office is leaning over her, talking to her. Jenny is looking up at him, and appears to be welcoming the attention. I'm disgusted with myself when I detect a faint hint of what might actually be jealousy. The bloke she is talking to is taller than me, better looking than me, wearing better clothes and is leaning against Jenny's computer monitor with the kind of nonchalant cool I would never be capable of. I feel like slapping myself across the face for thinking like this. Jenny has made it clear that she is interested in me, and I am the one who has constantly rebuffed her. I watch as he walks away, with Jenny still smiling. He walks over to some friends by the water cooler, presumably to say "I'm right up her cunt lads", or something of that nature. I look back at Jenny, who is taking a thick wad of chewed up paper out of her mouth. She picks up a ruler, places the paper on the tip of it, and flicks it through the air. It lands on the back of the bloke she has just been talking to, making a satisfyingly gross slapping sound as it does so. He feels it land, and turns around to be greeted by the sight of Jenny extending her middle finger and silently mouthing the words "stupid fucking twat" to him. He spends a few seconds making a pathetic attempt to arch his head around to investigate what is on his back, before heading towards the toilet. As I feel a broad grin spread across my face, a voice bellows into my left ear.

"Alright dude!" This is Danny's usual way of greeting me. Danny is someone who I happen to have been sat next to a few times since we finished our week of training and started taking calls (or since we "went live" as Richard laughably called it). Danny, in many ways, is the living embodiment of my worst nightmare. He's stupid, but not mean or nasty with it. He's loud, outgoing and confident, but not in an arrogant way. He's basically a well-meaning cretin. He's my worst nightmare because, although we have nothing in common, he appears to think that we do and, worse yet, appears to like me, and constantly seeks me out to attempt to engage me in the kind of inane banter that he is happy to fill his time with. His attempts to befriend me are clearly genuine, and this makes it difficult for me to hate him outright, or to be deliberately rude to him, but I do still find him intensely annoying. Such is his desire to form a friendship with me, he once even tried to conduct a conversation with me from opposite sides of a busy road, while we were walking in opposite directions. I suppose on the surface it might appear to him that there are some superficial similarities between us; we're the same age, both single and living in our own flat, all basic things that he could be forgiven for believing link us in some way. He doesn't realise that, beyond having blood in our veins, there is no common ground between us, or indeed me and anyone else. It's not Danny's fault. I simply have no contemporaries.

"How's things dude?" There's that word again. *"DUDE"*. He always uses it. I don't understand how people in this country have come to adopt that word so readily. We are Customer Service Advisors in the northwest of shitty old England, not a couple of surfers on some sun-drenched Californian beach. He has also called me "The Gazster" and, on one occasion, "The Gazinator".

"Fine, thank you," I answer.

"Did you watch the match last night?" I assume he's talking about football.

"Erm no, I didn't."

"Ah well you didn't miss much, it was shite anyway. We got battered."

It appears from his use of the word *we* that Danny has assumed we have another thing in common in supporting the same football team, but I see no reason to shatter this particular illusion.

"That's... unfortunate for us," I say, when I am alarmed by Richard's voice booming from right behind me.

"Gary!" he almost shouts at me, "what are you doing?"

"What does it look like I'm doing?" I ask, confused, "I was just talking to Danny."

"Yes well you're not being paid to talk to your friends; you're being paid to take calls."

I look up towards the service screen, which clearly shows that there are no calls waiting to come through, then back to Richard.

"But there aren't any calls queued. It's a bit quiet and I was just talking to Danny in between calls."

He makes a quick note of something on his clipboard.

"Well," he says, "I'm sure there are more constructive ways to be spending any time you have in between calls. Just try to concentrate and focus on the job you're paid to do please Gary."

"Jesus," Danny says after Richard is out of earshot, "he's really got it in for you hasn't he mate?"

Unfortunately, Danny is, on this occasion, absolutely correct. Richard has indeed been singling me out for this kind of petty treatment more and more over the last week or so, and it's beginning to get to me.

"You should report him or something," Jenny says later on in the canteen when I bring up the subject of Richard's continued harassment of me. Sitting with Jenny is something I've been doing more and more regularly. I seem able to be myself with her. It seems like she, more that any person I've met in probably the last decade, doesn't make me feel uncomfortable, and doesn't feel uncomfortable around me.

"I don't know about that, Jenny. I mean, who are the management or whoever more likely to side with? Someone who's just started here a couple of weeks ago, or an extreme jobsworth of a team leader who's been here for years?"

"I suppose so," she concedes.

"Plus, I don't think I have the mental strength for that kind of dispute anyway. Maybe if I gave even a bit of a shit about the job I could be bothered expending the energy on it, but I don't. I'll just get on with it, keep my head down and hope Richard gets bored with me and begins harassing someone else soon."

"Well he's a fucking prick. Someone needs to take the crater-faced little cock-sucker down a peg or two. Anyway," she says, obviously wanting to change the subject, "what are you doing tonight?"

"Nothing really," I reply, "just watching a film or something probably."

"Oh right, because I was wondering if you'd fancy coming to the pub or something?"

The idea of spending any more time in the company of my co-workers is not an appealing one.

"Erm, no thanks Jenny, I don't really feel like it," I say, trying to be as polite as I can. "Who's going, just a few of you from here?"

"Well actually," she says hesitantly, "I was hoping it'd be just me and you."

This is not what I was expecting.

"Oh," I say, "oh right. Well, thanks for asking, but like I said, I'm not really in the mood tonight."

"That's cool, maybe some other time?" She sounds disappointed, and I briefly consider changing my mind and accepting her offer, but think better of it. Part of me wants to, but girls like Jenny are pretty intimidating for a man like me. She's intelligent, confident, sexually liberated and unafraid to go after what she wants. Maybe if Jenny was a bit damaged in some way, if something had happened in her past to dent her confidence, I would contemplate going out with her, but the way she is, she's way out of my league.

Back at my desk, I've been on a call for almost ten minutes now. The caller is an elderly sounding gentleman called Mr Roberts. So far he has ordered a pair of slippers, a set of bath towels, a garlic crusher and a packet of embroidered handkerchiefs. A call like this should normally take between

104

three and four minutes. The reason this one has now taken well over twice that long is that Mr Roberts insists on making small talk between the ordering of each item. From the weather, to the news, to who he intends to give the garlic crusher to, to what he has planned for the day, no avenue of small talk has been left unexplored. Because I am being paid to be servile to these people, I am unable to simply hang up on him or tell him to fuck off. The dichotomy is that I am also expected to have a call like this wrapped up in less than five minutes, something Mr Roberts is making extremely difficult.

"Is that a Liverpool accent I detect, young man?"

"No. Birkenhead. It's sort of like Liverpool's idiotic half-brother."

"Oh I do love the Scouse sense of humour. And I've always been a big fan of the Beatles. Gerry Marsden too."

"Well, as I said, I'm from Birkenhead."

"How's the weather up where you are?" he asks me. "It's delightful down here."

"It's a bit hard for me to tell," I answer, "I'm working in a room without any windows."

"Oh well never mind," he says, his cheeriness undiminished, "I'm sure you'll make up for it when you finish. Out for a few pints with the lads I'll bet. I'm planning a bit of fishing myself later on."

"That sounds wonderful. Is there anything else I can help you with today Mr Roberts?"

I'm growing increasingly impatient now, not least because I know Richard will be aware of the call length, as any call over five minutes is flagged up on his computer screen, and he is now probably listening in on me, which means I also have to be very careful how I end the conversation. I don't want to give the little fucker any ammunition in his continuing crusade against me.

"Weeeeell, nothing I can think of, I – "

"In that case Mr Roberts I'd just like to thank you for your call and to wish you a very pleasant afternoon, goodbye."

Expertly done. I managed to cut him short without being rude, and even managed to use two of the three valedictions recommended in our training manuals. If Richard was listening in and monitoring me, I did everything by the book. Only the call length was a problem, and my stats are usually good enough that it would take a particularly petty person to pull me up on it. Of course, Richard is just such a person. I see him take off his headset and walk towards me. As he gets to my desk he doesn't stop, but walks right past.

"Watch your call length," he says to me as he drifts by, not even giving me a chance to respond. As I write up the sale details, it occurs to me how desperate Mr Roberts must have been for someone to talk to if he kept me on the line for so long. He sounded fairly elderly, and was perhaps a widower. His children may never visit, and maybe I am the only person he will speak to today. He went out of his way to be nice to me, and all I could think about was getting him off the phone. To him, I was a bit of human contact. To me, he was merely an inconvenience. Maybe I could have been nicer to him, made a bit more effort to reciprocate his attempts to make conversation, and in doing so made his day a little bit better.

"Fuck Mr Roberts," I think to myself, "I've got call stats to worry about."

I light up a cigarette as soon as I step out of the door, ignoring the hooting of a nearby car horn.

"Gary," I hear someone shout. I have no desire to find out who it is, so I keep my head down and keep walking. I can hear the car slowly following me slowly along the road, and again the shout comes:

"Gary, it's me."

I reluctantly stop and turn around, and am surprised to see my dad's head sticking out of the window of his car.

"Dad? What the fuck are you doing here? If you've taken to kerb crawling, Corporation Road is over that way."

"Get in son," he says.

A few of my co-workers are standing around outside, having a farewell chat, or waiting for lifts of their own, so I get into my dad's car rather than make a spectacle of myself.

"Oh, would you mind putting that out please?" Dad says, nodding towards the cigarette smouldering away in my right hand.

"Dad, I've only just lit it. You can't turn up unexpectedly like this, ask me to get into your car and then expect me to put my cigarette out."

"Please Gary, you know it's bad for my chest."

"Your chest? Dad, you're not Roy fucking Castle. You've got very mild asthma. A few minutes of second-hand smoke isn't gonna kill you."

"Gary..." he looks at me solemnly.

"Alright fine," I say, begrudgingly throwing it out of the window as Dad pulls away. "What are you doing here anyway?"

"I just thought I'd pick you up from work. I was in town anyway and knew you finished about this time. How was your day?"

"Abhorrent."

"That bad eh? Oh well, these things are sent to try us. You just have to pick yourself up after days like that and carry on regardless."

"What? What the hell is that supposed to mean?"

"Nothing son, I'm just saying, we all have bad days, and it's how you respond to them that is the important thing."

"Fucking hell Dad. 'These things are sent to try us'? 'Carry on regardless'? Are you capable of talking only in redundant clichés? Have you come here just to spout these homespun philosophies at me, or is there actually a real purpose to this little ambush?"

"Ambush? For God's sake Gary I..." he takes a breath before continuing "... it's not an ambush, I just wanted to pick you up so I could tell you... how proud me and your mother are of you. Making a go of this job, we know how difficult it is for you, but we're so pleased that you're making such an effort."

"Firstly, you have no idea how difficult it is for me. You aren't me; therefore you cannot possibly have any concept whatsoever how I feel about it either way, so please don't make those kinds of assumptions. I find it insulting. And secondly, I'm not 'making a go of it'. The only reason I come here is that I am basically forced to. I don't have a choice in the matter, and believe me, if I did, there is no fucking way on earth I would be coming here. So I'm very sorry, but the first sense of parental pride the two of you have ever felt is completely unfounded. I'm still the work-shy disappointment I was before. And I could have told you that anytime. I didn't need an un-requested lift home to avail myself of the opportunity."

Suddenly Dad steers the car over to the side of the road,

leans across me and opens the door.

"Get out," he says.

"I beg your fucking pardon?"

"I said get out of the bloody car."

"I certainly fucking won't! Why would you ask me to get out now?"

"Because I'm sick of it," he says, staring at the steering wheel, "I'm sick of you swearing at me. I'm sick of you talking to me and your mother as though we're idiots. I'm sick of your nihilistic attitude. I'm sick of every single nice gesture being thrown back in my face." He turns to look at me. "Now get out of my fucking car!"

"Not a fucking chance," I say as I close the door, "first you turn up uninvited at my workplace, then you badger me to get into the car, and now, thanks to the ridiculous route you've taken, I'm actually further away from home than I would have been if I had simply walked. So no, I won't get out of your car. The least you can do under the circumstances is finish what you set out to do and drive me home."

"OUT OUT OUT OUT OUT OUT!!!!!!!" Dad unclips my seat belt and starts shoving me towards the door, leaning across me to open it again. "Get the hell out of my car you little bastard, you can fucking walk home."

"Alright, alright," I say as I fend off his weak pushes with my arm, "I'll get out of the car."

Dad leans back in his seat and turns to look out of his window.

"All we ever did was try to do the right thing by you and your brother. All we ever wanted was for you both to be happy. And what have we got? A materialistic Tory-boy who barely manages to hide his contempt for us behind a mask of civility, and a second son who can't even be bothered to wear a mask of civility. What did we do that was so bad? Where did we get it so wrong?"

As he's talking I take my cigarettes from my pocket and quickly light one up. When he hears the click of the lighter, he turns towards me, to be greeted by a huge cloud of smoke being blown directly in his face.

"You little shit, get out!"

He finally manages to force me out of the car.

"Thanks for the fucking lift."
"Oh just........*fuck yourself,*" he shouts as I slam the door.

TWENTY

Throughout the trauma of my first weeks in the working world, I have felt the need to make an appointment with Brian, but my anger at his actions has outweighed this need, and I have resisted. Thanks to my growing uneasiness in this environment, resistance has proved increasingly difficult, and I have now finally, begrudgingly, relented. When I phoned his office, I was surprised to learn from his secretary that Brian had kept our regular weekly slot open for me since we last met. So, having informed work that I have a dental appointment, I once again visit the room where I have unloaded my darkest thoughts and secrets.

"This feels like a defeat for me."

"How do you mean?" asks Brian.

"Coming back here. It feels like I've thrown up the white flag. After what you did, I never wanted to see you again. I told myself I didn't need to see you again, but it's become increasingly obvious that that isn't the case. And I find that fucking humiliating."

"It's not a defeat Gary, if anything it's a very positive move on your part. In the past you came here because you were sent here. This is the first time that you've actually sought out my help. You're not throwing up a white flag, because I'm not the enemy, I want to help you. And on a more personal note, I'm very pleased to see you."

He pauses, presumably expecting me to reciprocate, but that's a bridge too far for me. It's one thing to come back here with my tail between my legs, but I'll be fucked if I'm gonna give him the satisfaction of knowing that it's actually quite a relief to see him too; albeit relief brought about by the fact that coming here on this day, at this time, is a reminder of a time, just weeks ago, when my life was considerably less complicated.

"So," he continues after tiring of waiting for me to speak, "would you like to start by telling me about the job you've been doing?"

"I've been working in a call centre, and it's every bit as pointless, boring and unrewarding as it sounds. My job title is 'Customer Service Advisor'. Fuck knows who came up with that title but it pretty much sums it up."

"And how have things been going?"

"How do you think they've been going? Every bit as horrifically as I knew full well they would."

"What particular problems have you encountered?"

"Well for one I'm surrounded, for the most part, by trenchant buffoons. That applies to the customers who I have to speak to and, especially, the people I work with. Seriously, they're just fucking idiots. These are people whose main topics of conversation are who's being voted off *I'm A Celebrity*. I'd never even heard of that show till I started there, now it's all I fucking hear about. People whose cultural references don't extend beyond *Call the fucking Midwife*. This is the type of person you have exposed me to. *Cretins*. Each and every one of the fuckers. The managers and team leaders are even worse. There's this one particular fuckwit called Richard. It's not just the fact that he's an idiot, and the fact that he seems to have made it his life's work to make things as difficult for me as he possibly can, it's how seriously he takes himself, how seriously he takes his job. You'd think he was a missionary, converting savages to Christianity, or a scientist on the verge of finding a cure for cancer. None of them realise how petty and inconsequential the work they're doing is. None of them realise that every single one of them is living their life on the precipice of complete psychological collapse, and it's like all they can do to stave it off is to throw themselves mind, body and soul into these stupid jobs. As though opening their eyes for a second and seeing how pointless it all is will push them over the brink. It's just fucking pathetic. Not that my life has any meaning of course. But at least my eyes are open to the fact. And as if all that wasn't enough, I'm now earning less then I was when I was receiving benefits. This session with you is costing me about a day's wages, even with the discount you've given me. So you'd better say something worthwhile for once."

Brian nods along, making notes as I talk. I wonder why he's making notes as I talk about other people, and whether this indicates that, all the time I have been coming to see him, he has just been on auto-pilot, and has just been doodling or scribbling absent-mindedly in his book. Perhaps if I were to grab his notebook, it would be full of nothing but solitary games of hangman or noughts and crosses.

"Look Brian, just stop your fucking doodling for a minute and answer a question for me."

"Certainly Gary, what would you like to ask me?"

"Could you forget your professional vanity and accept that you've made a bad judgement call?"

"A bad judgement call about what?"

"What the fuck do you think? About sending me to work. Isn't it blindingly obvious, even to someone with your lack of insight, that forcing me to sit behind a computer desk, answering telephones, being surrounded by the living fucking dead, is of absolutely no benefit whatsoever to me or to anyone else? All this job has done for me is increase my anxiety, and significantly increase my alcohol intake. You've tried a little experiment, and it hasn't worked. You've exercised your power by turning my life inside out, just to satisfy your own curiosity, and your hypothesis has been proven wrong. So instead of using me to make yourself feel somehow omnipotent, maybe you can just buy an ant farm or something instead, sign me back off work, and we'll all be a lot better off."

Brian puts his notebook down.

"Gary, I never thought that this was going to be easy for you. I never thought things would improve overnight. But I'm confident that you will come through this a better person. I think it's important for you to focus less on the lives of other people, and to concentrate on your own progress. And, unfortunately Gary, you will always run into people like Richard. No matter what walk of life you are in, there will always be people who make things difficult for you. The challenge is finding a way to deal with such things. But surely this doesn't apply to everyone there. I mean, they can't all be that bad. Have you actually made any friends?"

"Not friends as such, but there's a couple of people there I sort of get on with."

"OK well tell me about them, what are their names?"

"Well when I say a couple, there's only really one. Her name's Jenny."

"Oh, a girl?" Brian asks, suddenly animated.

"Yes, don't get too excited, there's nothing going on. But she's... nice, I suppose. I mean, she's the first person I've met in about a decade that doesn't think I'm weird. Well, maybe she

112

does think I'm weird, but if she does she doesn't seem to mind. She actually seems to want to listen to me. Not that I've particularly got anything of interest to say, but she... just likes to listen. And she's funny too, and she thinks I'm funny as well, which is a bit weird."

"Do you think she's attracted to you?"

"I suppose so," I say after a long pause, "not that I'm likely to be a good judge of that, but a few people have said she fancies me. And she always makes a point of sitting by me, and she has asked me out for a drink a couple of times. She's not exactly shy so, yeah I suppose I'd have to say that for some bizarre reason, she is attracted to me."

"And do you reciprocate?"

"Let's not get carried away here Brian," I say defensively, "just because I don't dislike the girl, doesn't mean I'm ready for that sort of thing. Like I said, she's a nice girl, and yes I suppose she is attractive, but that's a step I'm not ready to take yet. But..."

"But what, Gary?" Brain asks

"Ok, now I don't want you to read too much into this, but I did have a dream about her the other night."

"I see. And would you like to describe the dream to me?"

"Don't start getting a fucking hard-on Brian. It wasn't a sex dream or anything. My memories of it are a bit hazy, but basically it involved me and Jenny. We were in the call centre, but there was only me and her in there. We were doing exactly the same job we always do. We were answering calls, writing up sales and all the mind-numbingly boring, glaringly pointless stuff we do every day. Then suddenly, we stood up and began singing a duet."

"A duet?" Brian repeats, clearly as surprised at where this dream is going as I was. "What was the duet?"

"It was 'What Have I Done to Deserve This?' by the Pet Shop Boys with Dusty Springfield." Brian looks perplexed.

"I'm unfamiliar with that particular song," he says.

"Trust me, you're not missing out."

"I have a Dusty Springfield album, well a compilation, but I've never heard of the Pet Shop Boys."

"They're a pop duo. They're still going now I think, but they were big in the 80s, but it's not really that important is it?"

"Did they sing that song 'The King of Wishful Thinking'?"

"No, that was Go West. They were a duo too, but the Pet Shop Boys were more electro. Look Brian, do you want to hear this fucking dream, or do you intend to waste my money talking about shit pop music?"

"Yes, you're right Gary, please continue," he urges, clearly riveted.

"Right, so we stand up and break into this song. And I mean it's the whole shebang. It's got a fucking choreographed dance routine and everything, and the stupid fucking headsets we have to wear every day turn into these radio microphone things, and we're both singing passionately into them, and we go through the entire song. I'd be hard pushed to quote you a single full line of lyrics from it now, but in this dream I know every single word, and so does Jenny."

"And then what happened?" Brian asks without looking up from the notebook he's been scribbling in the whole time.

"Nothing happens. That's it. The song finishes, we sit back down, and the call centre is full again. The sound of synth-heavy pop music is replaced by the usual background office hum of ringing phones and chattering voices."

Brian puts his pen down and the taut leather of his chair squeaks as he leans back in it before asking the inevitable question:

"And what do you think this dream means?"

"Oh fuck off Brian, it doesn't mean a single fucking thing. It's just a dream. Now, if you're asking me if I believe that dreams are results of the subconscious, or manifestations of unknown desires or anxieties then I'd say yes, on occasion they are. But most of the time they're completely meaningless, just nonsense, and this is one of the nonsensical ones. Yes it's unusual but dreams by their very nature are a bit unusual. Didn't I tell you not to read too much into it before I described it to you?"

I don't need Brian or anyone else to tell me that the reason for my defensive tone is clear. Deep down I know that I'm in denial about Jenny. The more time I've been spending in her company, the more I've come to enjoy it. If I was being completely honest with Brian I'd tell him that she's the one thing that makes my job almost bearable, the one thing that stops me from going insane in that place (along with the small bottles of whisky and vodka I've taken to smuggling into work in my bag). And I'd also tell him that I do have something approaching genuine feelings for her. But that's a hard thing for me to admit to myself, never mind to anyone else. It's very strange for me to be having feelings at all, and I'm embarrassed and ashamed by them. They seem weak, obscene and wrong to me. Maybe I should be honest with Brian about this; after all, I have been honest about just about everything else, but for now these feelings are something I need to come to terms with myself before I can think about vocalising them.

"Fair enough, but the way you've spoken about this girl is a significant development for you, I think. I'm not going to push the matter, but I'll simply say that when you speak about this Jenny, you're voice takes on a certain tone of optimism that I've never heard from you before, and I really do find that very encouraging. Now, before you shout me down I'll let that particular topic lie. Is there anything else in particular you want to talk about? "

"Actually, there is one problem," I reply, "there's this other woman there, this older trainer called Ruth."

"What's the problem with her?"

"She keeps trying to... touch me. It's obvious what she's after, but I don't know how to deal with it. She's quite high up the chain of command in that place, and I don't know what to say to put her off without provoking her to try and make life difficult for me. I've got enough to worry about with that stupid bastard Richard without having another one turn against me."

"Hmmm, it's quite a delicate situation, but there's only really one way for you to deal with it. The next time that she does something like that, you simply inform her that, while you are very flattered, you are just not interested, and that her advances make you feel uncomfortable. Tell her that you consider workplace romances to be inappropriate and that you wish to keep your relationship strictly professional."

"Ok, I'll try that."

"But be sure to be as tactful as possible. You know what they say: 'Hell hath no fury like a woman scorned'."

"I really wouldn't know, but thanks for the advice. It's probably about the first helpful thing you've ever said to me. I think I'm gonna go now Brian."

"That's fine Gary. I'm glad you came here today. I honestly feel that, although you may not think it, you are making real progress. Please feel free to call me at any time."

"I'll be sure to do that if I need someone to point out the blindingly obvious for me."

I return to work the following day, with Brian's advice about a tactful abnegation of Ruth's overtures at the forefront of my mind, which is just as well, as it seems Ruth has made it her mission to seduce me today. Every time she walks past my desk I can see her staring at me. I keep my eyes firmly on my computer screen but I can practically feel her eyes burning into me. The one time I accidentally make eye contact with her she gives me what she presumably thinks is a flirtatious and arousing wink, but which only makes her look like she's having a petit-mal seizure. I know that it is only a matter of time before she makes her move, so I practise a subtle rebuffing of her advances over and over in my head. I have it all worked out. I imagine several possible scenarios and locations where she will make her move. I assume it will be when I'm away from my desk, probably in a corridor on my way to or from the canteen. Somewhere a bit secluded, that's for sure. Nothing prepares me then, for the method she employs. I've just finished a call when I hear her voice behind me.

"Hello Gary," she says, having for some reason adopted the husky voice of a telephone sex line operative.

"Hello Ruth," I reply in as deadpan a voice as I can manage. I don't want to be giving this woman any ideas by appearing too friendly. It appears to do no good however, as she assumes her usual position of leaning over me, her breasts uncomfortably close to my face, with her hand resting on my knee. I look around the crowded office and everyone seems completely oblivious to what is transpiring before them. They either don't know or don't care that one of their colleagues is currently falling victim to a particularly unsubtle case of sexual harassment. I want to yell out to them for help, but feel paralysed with fear. Ruth, meanwhile, seems to be revelling in my discomfort. I feel totally helpless. She is the hunter and I am her quarry. Her hand slides further up my leg. I search the recesses of my mind for my rehearsed speeches but find nothing. Cold sweat drips down my back as her hand edges yet further up my leg,

116

until the tip of her finger actually comes into contact with the tip of my dick.

"RUTH!" I say indignantly as I stand up, banging my knees on the desk and knocking my bottle of water to the floor, "this is highly inappropriate behaviour. I am very flattered by your advances, but would be most grateful if, in future, you could keep your hands away from the vicinity of my genitals."

Ruth is looking up at me from her semi-crouched position with a look of abject horror. She looks to her right and I follow her eyes to see the entire room staring at us. She turns her head back in my direction, to realise her face is about six inches away from my groin. Somewhere, in an unseen corner, someone starts to laugh. Then another laughs, then a third. Ruth stands up, mutters something about a meeting and scurries out of the room. By now pretty much everyone in the office is laughing at me. I run towards the main exit, tripping over a stray wire as I go. I get outside and light up a cigarette with a trembling hand. I try to control my hyperventilating with the breathing techniques Brian has shown me. Running through about ten of my rhythmical processes eventually calms me down sufficiently to avert a full-blown panic attack, but nothing can change the fact that, yet again, I have found myself humiliated in front of a large group of idiots. On the other hand, at least I need no longer live in fear of Ruth's advances.

TWENTY-ONE

From: angryloner@hotmail.com
To: sportseditor@guardian.co.uk
Subject: Britain's gradual slide into the abyss

From a conversation I overheard earlier today:

"So I turns round and I says to him, 'Yeah? Well that's not my problem is it?' And then he turns round and says to me, 'Yeah? Well maybe I'm making it your problem'. So then I'm like..."

At this point I managed to block out this banal and directionless conversation. I think I placed my hands over my ears and closed my eyes, though I wanted to push a biro into my auditory canal. I don't even know where to start on this little exchange; the superfluous uses of "yeah" and "like", or the fact that everyone seems to conduct conversations these days whilst in a constant state of rotation.

Mr Sports Editor, I think you probably know who this is, so I shall waste no time on introductions. You should know by now that you cannot avoid me simply by blocking my email accounts. If I have a point I wish to make to you, then I shall have my say, regardless.

I have not been in touch with you for a while, and I have decided that it is now time for me to correspond once more. I have a lot of news for you, most of it bad. Things have got far worse for me since I last wrote. I have been forced, against my will, to enter the world of the working. The job into which I have been forced is that of "Customer Service Advisor" in a call centre. I wasn't even aware that such places existed before I had to work in one, but how like modern Britain it is that we have them. What is so wrong with this country that we actually think we need these places? Is it so essential that someone be able to order a set of dinner table place mats at 9pm on a Saturday night? Or check their bank account balance at 7am on a Wednesday morning? Would our lives really fall apart if we couldn't do these things? If the people of Britain could see the insides of one of these hell holes, with hundreds of people gradually being turned into robots as they are forced to repeat the same scripted customer service spiel over and over and over again, their brains slowly ceasing to work at full capacity due to the lack of stimulation, their eyes straining and heads aching from staring at computer screens all day, well, I hope that it would fill them with shame for having created the need for these places to exist, and drive them to find their nearest one, and burn it to the ground.

When I was sent to work in this place, certain people thought it would be an education for me, that I would learn something. Well I have learned something Mr Sports Editor. I have learned that I was right all along. I have always suspected that this nation was filled with idiots and bores. In recent weeks, I have come into contact with more people than I care to count, both in person and via the telephone, and everything I have learned has confirmed my suspicions. When whoever it was said "Modern Life is Rubbish", he didn't know the fucking half of it.

Well, I have nothing further to add. I hope you have taken the time to read this message in its entirety. I am aware that you are very likely to now block this email address, but I want to assure you that I will be in touch again very soon.

Regards,
Anonymous.

P.S. I saw a piece of graffiti the other day. Someone had written it in their own faeces on the wall of one of the toilet cubicles in my workplace. It said, simply, *"FUCK OFF"*. Inarticulate perhaps, but somehow, it just sums it all up.

TWENTY-TWO

"… I ordered these items three bloody weeks ago now, and still no sign of them. I mean, what the bloody hell are you people playing at? Are you all complete imbeciles?"

Mr Rodwell from West Haddon is an angry man. Or at least, he is today. The cause of this anger is the order he placed with us some time ago, which has yet to be dispatched from our warehouse. Clearly he is unable to function without his egg poacher and wicker washing basket.

"Mr Rodwell, please calm down, I'm sure—"

"Don't you tell me to calm down young man. You sods have taken my money from me, and haven't sent me a bloody thing. No phone calls, no emails, nothing to tell me what the hell is going on with my order, why the hell should I calm down?"

A quick peek over the top of my computer monitor confirms that Richard is away from his desk, which means nobody is listening in to my call.

"You companies are all the bloody same," continues Mr Rodwell, "perfectly happy to take our money, but when it comes to customer care, you couldn't give a shit – "

"Shut your fucking mouth," I say quietly.

"I beg your par—"

"If we were standing face to face, would you dare to talk to me like that?"

"Well… I …"

"No you fucking wouldn't. Because if you did, Mr Rodwell, I would rip your fucking face off. Just because I'm at the end of a phone line, you think you have some sort of advantage over me you pathetic piece of shit. Well I've got an advantage over you. I have your home address on screen in front of me. I know exactly where you live. I have your credit card details. All you know about me is my first name, which could be made up for all you know. If I hear one more abusive word from you, I will use that advantage. I might use your credit card to sign you up to a kiddie porn website, or to book myself a nice fucking holiday. Maybe I'll just make a nice fat contribution to a few charities. "

"Can I speak to a supervisor please?"

"No you fucking can't. You don't get to speak to anyone but

me you miserable fucking bastard. Now let me tell you what's going to happen. In a moment, I am going to end this call, and then you will wait patiently, for as long as it fucking takes, for your order to arrive. Even if it takes years. Even if it takes decades. Even if it takes until the end of fucking time. And you will never call this number again. And if I find out that you have, I will be sending you something in the post that you really won't want to receive. And you can be sure it'll get to you a lot quicker than this fucking order of yours. Now Mr Rodwell, fuck right off, and thank you for your call."

Above the door to the main office is an elaborate plaque, emblazoned with a quote form Theodore Roosovelt: "Far and away the best prize that life has to offer is the chance to work hard at work worth doing." It's probably the stupidest quote I have ever heard, made doubly stupid when used in the context of this shithole call centre. I am not a conscientious worker. I have no inclination to give of my best when I come in to work, which is why at the end of the day, having first ensured the coast is clear, I have no qualms about simply hanging up on a customer mid-order when it appears their call will drag on past four o'clock. I'm clearing up at my work station when Jenny comes over and sits in the empty chair next to me.

"So Gary," she says, "what are you up to tonight then?"

I'd get no prizes for guessing where this line of questioning is leading. I've already politely refused her offers to go out for a drink on two occasions, so she's probably hoping it'll be third time lucky for her today. Part of me really wants to be ready to accept her offer, but even though I may want to go for a drink with Jenny, the prospect of actually doing it is a huge and terrifying step that I don't think I am yet ready to take. I consider lying, and telling her that I already have plans for tonight, but I think I've already established myself in the minds of my colleagues as the type of person who rarely, if ever, has "plans".

"Erm, I'm not really up to anything tonight. Unless you consider watching TV and getting slightly drunk on my own to be doing something."

"Well then, why don't you come out for a drink with me tonight, and we'll both get slightly drunk together?"

It would be so easy to just accept. So easy to say "OK" or "that'd be delightful". At least, it would be for most people, but for me, the easier thing is to not take the plunge, and to spend yet another evening alone.

"Thanks for the offer Jenny," I say apologetically, "but I've had a bit of a shitty day and I'd rather—"

"All the more reason for you to come out for a few drinks with me then," Jenny interrupts.

"Really Jenny, I—"

"Look Gary," she says, cutting me short again. She leans in closer and lowers her voice a little, "you've already knocked me back twice, please don't tell me you're gonna do it a third time. I'm not gonna take an overdose or slit my wrists in the bath if you don't come for a drink with me, but there is a limit to the amount of rejection I'm prepared to put up with. I'm not a fucking idiot, so I can clearly sense that some part of you wants to, and I won't be asking you again if you say no this time, so think carefully before you respond. I'm not asking you to fucking marry me, just to come for a few drinks, and you can leave any time you want. You can even choose which pub we go to."

This time I really am left with no way out. If she is being this persistent, then resistance is clearly futile. Plus, I can't help but admire the girl's tenacity, and I'm also very flattered that a girl like Jenny would pursue someone like me with such determination.

"OK you're right. How about the Crown? At about seven?"

"There, that wasn't so fucking hard was it," she replies, perking up considerably, "I'll see you then."

I make my way home and get showered and changed. While getting dressed I wonder to myself, "Is this a date?" If it is, then I think it's the first one I've had in at least four years, and that was an abortive disaster, having been persuaded, under duress, to go for a drink with a friend of Aimee's. The writing was on the wall when I rejected her salutary kiss on the cheek, explaining to her that it wasn't personal, just that, as a stranger, I could not vouch for her personal hygiene and feared the germs that could be passed on by her. About fifteen minutes later, she made some excuse about a sudden family emergency and left, much to my relief, and I hadn't even been close to going on a date since. Jesus. Four years, that's a long fucking time by anyone's standards. Even mine. I hadn't realised just how long it had actually been. This train of thought begins to make me a little anxious, so I tell myself that it's not a date, it's just two friends – not even friends really, more like work colleagues – going out for a drink, nothing more than that. I check my watch and see that I have an hour to spare. If I'm going out drinking, I should probably eat something first. As I walk into my kitchen something strange occurs to me. I realise that, for the last few days, I have barely eaten a morsel. I check through my fridge and cupboards and find several items of food that have gone off, untouched since I bought them. This is something that never happens to me, I have never been a waster of food, and my appetite is just about the one thing about me that has always remained healthy. I try to remember the last time I made myself a proper meal, but struggle to do so, remembering only the odd mouthful here and there. I also notice that my jeans are a little loose, and have to force another hole into my belt with a knife. I recall having had to do the same with the belt from my work trousers a couple of days ago too. It seems that, as well as increasing my drinking, the stress from having to work is also suppressing my appetite and causing significant weight loss. Still, I know I should try and eat something now, rather than drink on an empty stomach, so I make myself a small sandwich. I sit down to eat it but I have absolutely no appetite. I try to force it down my throat anyway, but it takes me nearly half an hour to get barely halfway through it. By this time it's getting very close to seven, so I leave the rest of the sandwich uneaten and walk to the pub.

When I arrive I am relieved to see that Jenny is already there and the pub is pretty quiet. I walk towards the table Jenny has secured for us, and I am taken aback when she, by way of a greeting, stands up and kisses me on the cheek.

"Hiya Gary," she says friendlily. I buy myself a pint and sit down across from her, positioning myself so that I can see the rest of the pub, of course.

"I wasn't sure whether you'd actually come or not," Jenny continues.

"No, I'd said I'd come. I wouldn't just not show up."

"No, but you weren't exactly enthusiastic about accepting my invite though were you?"

"No I suppose I wasn't. I'm sorry about that. It's not that I didn't want to, I just have trouble... being social. I'm just not a sociable person," I say by way of a lame explanation.

"Apparently fucking not," Jenny says, "so I'm really glad you came."

"Mind you, I suppose not being sociable is one of the nicer things that have been said about me in work."

"What do you mean?" she asks.

"Come on Jenny, it's pretty obvious that most people in that place think I'm pretty fucking weird."

"Well, yeah. To be honest a few of them do," she concedes.

"I'm just... I just can't pretend to be like them. Or pretend that I do like them. I can't just adapt the way some people can. I know most people don't like their work colleagues, but most people can fake it. Even if I wanted to do that, I wouldn't know how. Every time I overhear one of their stupid discussions I just feel like ramming my head through my computer screen, or drowning myself in the water cooler. And I know they all pick up on how out of place I feel around them, and on the way that I can't just join in with them. They don't seem to consider the possibility that they're the ones who should feel embarrassed by the way they are, so they just think I'm weird. Which I think is why I've been so hesitant to come out with you. I know what most people think of me in there, and I suppose I just can't quite get my head around why you'd want to be associated with me. I mean, you could probably have your pick of the lads in there, but it's me that you've been asking out. And they must think you're a bit odd for showing any kind of interest in me."

"But I don't give a fuck about what they think. I like *you* Gary. I don't know why exactly, I mean the fact that you're pretty fucking fit might have something to do with it." I feel myself blush, and Jenny notices too and gives a little smile before going on. "But it's more than just that. There's just something about you I find you interesting."

"Interesting?" I say with amazement. "*Interesting*? Jenny, I'm 29 years old, and I spend the vast majority of my time alone. My idea of a good time is spending an entire day cleaning my flat. My family are embarrassed by me. I only have three friends in the entire world, and I'm not even sure how much I like them. The only job I've ever had could literally be performed by a

124

monkey, and I haven't had a girlfriend for... well, for an extremely long time. What on earth could you possibly find interesting about me?"

"Well, I think it's mainly the fact that there's more to you than you present to everyone. All the other lads in work, yeah some of them are fit and everything, but there's nothing more to them than that. And frankly I find them all fucking boring. I think what I find most interesting about you though, is the fact that you're a better person than you really let on to people. I think maybe you're a better person even than you realise yourself. I think there's a really clever, witty, nice guy trapped inside you, and for whatever reason, you just don't seem to want to let him out."

"You're wrong about me Jenny. There's nothing more to me than what's on the surface. There's no substance to me. I'm basically just a weird twat."

"I disagree with you Gary. I think there's a lot more to you than meets the eye, and I wouldn't be wasting my time with you if I thought there wasn't. Don't get me wrong, you can be a real smart arse sometimes, which people can find really annoying, including me, and I'm sure you're capable of being a bit of a weird twat too, and I do wish you'd crack even just a bit of a fucking smile occasionally, but nobody's perfect."

This is a lot for me to take in. I'm pretty sure my reaction to Jenny's remarks would be fairly caustic if they came from anyone else. I would have been offended at the presumptions, and scathing of the attempt at amateur psychology. But somehow, I can accept it coming from her. I've only been here a quarter of an hour and I've already had more compliments and affection than I've had in long while. Not that I'm complaining or being self-pitying regarding that. I'm well aware that this is almost entirely of my own choosing.

After this initial intensity, our conversation settles down a little. We spend the next couple of hours just talking and drinking. We slag off some of the people in work, especially Richard, we discuss what films and music we like. I explain some of my mental health issues to her, and she is empathetic and understanding without a hint of condescension. She even pretends to be interested in one of my denunciations of modern Britain. All the kinds of things I suppose normal people do on normal dates. Not that this is an actual date; and I realise something strange. During all this time, through all this conversation, I've been doing something that is pretty much anathema to me. I've been looking Jenny square in the eye almost constantly. My gaze has left hers for barely a minute. Closing time creeps up on us, and suddenly it's time for us to leave.

"Come on," says Jenny as she finished the last of her drink, "you can walk me to the taxi rank."

We walk around the corner towards the row of cab's waiting outside Park Taxis. As we do so, I sense that Jenny might want to hold my hand. What really surprises me though, is the fact that I actually wouldn't mind if she did, maybe I even want her to.

"Ok, well thanks for walking me to the cab," Jenny says, "I'm off work for a few days now, I'm going down to London to see some friends, but I'll see you next week I suppose?"

"Yeah, see you in work," I say. I am about to say goodnight when something happens that I am completely unprepared for. Jenny takes a step towards me, grabs me around the neck and kisses me passionately. I hesitate initially, standing there like a mannequin. This doesn't deter Jenny though, and as she continues to kiss me I nervously move my hands up and around her waist. She kisses me harder as I do this, and presses her breasts into my chest. I feel my heart pounding against them. I slide my hands down onto Jenny's arse and squeeze it tightly. The average human mouth contains forty three different types of bacteria, but for now I forget that as Jenny moves her tongue inside my mouth, twisting and swirling it around mine. I feel my cock getting hard and press it against Jenny's front. She feels it against her and moves her hand down to it and rubs it hard through my jeans. It feels incredible. Every single nerve in my body seems to tingle, and I remember the first time I ever masturbated. I feel the same mystifying euphoria, the same uniquely intimidating sense of discovery, as though I was the first person on the planet to ever experience this, and now that I had, not really knowing what to do about it. I want to push Jenny against the wall and fuck her right there and then. I want to do every lustful thing that everyone else does. I want to suck her tits and taste her cunt. I want her mouth around my cock. I want to

126

fill her with my come. I want to feel her insides wrapped tightly around my cock as I fuck her and fuck her and fuck her. And I want to do it all without losing eye contact with her for a second. I want to surrender to sex. To sex with Jenny. I know I can't. I know I won't. But at least I want to. Suddenly Jenny stops kissing me and pulls her head back.

"Come back to mine with me Gary," she pleads.

"I don't know Jenny," I say.

"Please Gary, we don't have to do anything, just come and spend the night with me."

I want to, I can't believe I'm thinking this but I actually do want to. But I know that I won't. It doesn't matter how much I'd like to; such a long time spent sleeping alone means it'll be too big a step for me to take so soon.

"I'm sorry Jenny, I want to, I really do want to but I can't. I've... I've been on my own for so long, and I'm just not ready yet. But I think I want to be. Believe me Jenny, there's no greater compliment I can pay you than the fact that I really want to be able to spend the night with you. But it's just too soon, I'm sorry."

"It's OK," she says smiling, "I didn't really think you would, but I really want to see you again. Like this I mean, outside of work. Away from all those fuckwits."

"I want to too," I say. And I mean it.

"When I get back from London, we should do this again. I'd better go anyway, that taxi driver's probably getting a bit impatient by now. Well, either that or he's wanking over us. Goodnight Gary."

"Goodnight Jenny," I say. She kisses me hard on the mouth, walks away and jumps into the waiting cab.

I consider taking a cab home myself, but it's a clear evening and there's nobody around, so I decide to walk home instead. I walk up through Hamilton Square, with its Georgian architecture, Grade 1 listed buildings, and homeless people sleeping in the gardens. I pass the top of Price Street, the site of one of the first synagogues on Merseyside, now the site of the completely empty Bar 54 nightclub. I pass Sherlock's nightclub, where the only thing louder than the awful music blaring out is the sound of three men arguing with the bouncers outside. I walk through the bus station, past a bunch of teenagers pulling wheelies on their bikes. I hear them shouting abuse at me, keep my head down and keep walking. I walk past the boarded-up Blockbuster, through the car park where there is a man pissing against the pay-and-display machine. He looks up at me, and again I keep my eyes on the ground and I keep moving. Past the hideous bars and pubs, avoiding eye-contact with the smokers outside, past the kebab shop and the curry houses. Past the tiny shops that will unlock your phone for you, past the pound shops, the empty shops and those that will soon be empty.

Despite all this filth, and despite the permanent sense of danger, I find the long stroll home invigorating. It gives me time to mull over what has just happened with Jenny. I can still taste her saliva in my mouth. I've been trying not to swallow it, so I can savour it. The more I think about it, the more positive I feel. Jenny is the only person I've met in years who I actually find remotely interesting. She's the only person in years who doesn't simply walk away when I open my mouth. She's the only person in the shithole they call Park Communications who isn't a complete idiot. She's the only girl in a very very long time that I've actually fancied. Jesus, I actually fancy someone. I'm actually feeling basic human attraction, and I feel OK about it. In fact, I feel pretty fucking good about it.

As I turn into my street, something catches my attention in the corner of my eye. I notice an odd fluttering motion at the foot of the first wall on the street. I look down and see, cowering against the wall, huddled in the darkness, a pigeon. I stop and look at it for a moment, expecting it to fly away. Then I realise the fluttering I noticed was the pigeon attempting to do just that. It is flapping its right wing, but the left remains still. I look a little closer and see the left wing is wounded, and one of its eyes is missing. Presumably one of the many cats on the street has attacked it, but been disturbed before it could finish the job. Or maybe it happened further away than this. Perhaps the pigeon managed to fly away from its attacker, but was unable to make it any further, crash landed here, and has sought some sort of pathetic refuge against the wall of this house, and is now hoping against hope that it will recover enough to fly away before another cat comes along and puts it out of its misery. I stare at the animal for what must be several minutes, wondering what I should do. I am no animal lover. All animals do is cover you in fur and make you sneeze, but this is no way for any creature to die, alone and afraid. But on the other hand, who am I to interfere with the laws of nature? Plus, if I do decide to intervene in any way, I will have to put my hands on an animal that is naturally very unclean to begin with, and is no doubt considerably more so having been ravaged in this way. The urge to help it and the urge to walk on by fight a brief battle within me, and the urge to walk on by emerges victorious.

I walk just a few steps towards my house when the pigeon emits a plaintive "cooing" sound. Now, I have no idea whether this sound is meaningless or is the result of my walking away, but it feels to me like a desperate plea for help, and I find myself unable to walk on. I turn back to the bird, and know that I must try to help. I kneel down beside it, and place a hand either side of it, ready to pick it up. I attempt to block out the thoughts of contamination and begin to close my hands around it. Just as I make contact, though, the pigeon panics and begins to frantically flap its one healthy wing. I pick the struggling bird up, but its aggressive flapping proves too much for me and it slips from my half-hearted grip. The bird hits the floor and waddles back to face the wall. I make another attempt to scoop it up, doing so more gently now, but again the animal fails to understand what I am trying to do, and struggles free. Instead of heading back to the wall this time, it walks towards the gap between the fence of the house and that of the house next door. The gap between the two fences is just wide enough for the bird to fit in. I know that if it gets more than an arms length between them, I will be unable to reach it and its fate will be sealed.

"Please," I say as gently as I can, trying to imitate the kind of voice people use when trying to gain the trust of an animal, "let me help you." But it evades my attempts to block its path, running between my legs and between the fences, where it settles down with its back end towards me, presumably believing it has found some from of sanctuary. I kneel down by the fences, roll my shirt sleeve up and try to reach it. Every time I get near it though, the dumb animal edges further away from me.

"For fucks sake," I shout at it, "let me help you. Why won't you let me help you?"

At this point the pigeon turns its head to face me and, with its one remaining eye, looks me square in the face.

"Please," I say, quietly this time, "please let me help you." As I say this, I feel something moist on my face, and notice a strange salty taste in my mouth. I put a finger to my cheek and wipe off a clear liquid, and realise that I've started crying. There's no doubt about it. The taste in my mouth is unmistakable. It may have been a long, long time since I tasted my own tears, but even now the taste is instantly recognisable. I look back to the pigeon, which has been watching me this whole time. As it stares back at me I begin to cry harder. Then, as it turns away from me, I begin to weep uncontrollably. The tears stream down my face. I haven't cried like this since I was a child. In fact, I'm not sure if I have ever cried like this. But now, it seems like 29 years' worth of suppressed emotion is all coming out. My entire body shakes and my eyes sting with the endless flow of tears. I try again to grab the pigeon, but this time it moves completely out of my reach.

"*PLEASE,*" I scream at it, "*PLEASE LET ME HELP YOU.*"

But I know it's no use, the bird is beyond my grasp, and it will now almost certainly die here, wedged between these two fences. I drop face down onto the floor, screaming and banging the pavement until my fists begin to bleed. I smash my forehead against the concrete, nearly knocking myself out cold, screaming as loudly as I can to stop myself losing consciousness. The curtains in the two houses begin to twitch, and I run back to my flat and cry myself to sleep.

It's still early when I awake. I take a plastic bag from my kitchen and walk back to where I left the pigeon. As I suspected, it is still there, but has clearly been dead for a few hours. Somehow, before dying, it has managed to turn itself around and move a little closer to the street, so I can reach between the fences with the bag wrapped around my hand and pick the bird's lifeless body up. I cover it up with the bag and carry it round to the small grassy patch of land behind my flat. Using a piece of wood I dig down about a foot into the ground, and place the dead bird, wrapped inside the bag, in the hole before covering it back up. I stand over the shallow grave, and feel as though I should say something.

"Goodbye" is the only thing I can think of. I turn back towards my flat to get ready for work.

It turns out that burying a dead pigeon in a shallow grave sets the tone for my day. The impromptu funeral delays my usual morning routine and before I even leave my flat, I know I'm going to be late. I run at least half the way there, and what is usually a half hour walk is completed in less than fifteen minutes, which is still long enough for me to be five minutes late. I pause as I get to the glass doors.

"Once more unto the fucking breach," I say to my reflection.

I run up the stairs to the main office with sweat dripping from me. My hopes of avoiding Richard are dashed as soon as I reach my desk.

"You're late Gary," he says after performing his usual trick of appearing behind me, seemingly from nowhere. I turn around to plead my case and Richard looks me up and down with a look of disgust.

"And you look a mess."

I put my hands into my pocket to hide my bloodied knuckles.

"I only look a mess," I say between panting breaths, "because I ran practically the whole way here so I wouldn't be late."

"Well," he says barely suppressing a smile, "it was all for nothing, because you are late. If you're late again this month that'll be an official warning."

"What is your problem Richard?" I ask, beginning to lose my temper. "Did I do something terrible to you in a previous life that makes you feel the need to pick at me like this? Does it make you feel better about yourself somehow?"

"I have no idea what you mean Gary," he says, feigning bemusement, "I'm just trying to manage my team as well as I can. If you feel that I'm picking at you, then maybe you shouldn't be giving me so much reason to. If your work and conduct were up to scratch, then I wouldn't have cause to speak to you like this would I?"

As usual, he walks away from me before I can think of a clever comeback, and I turn back to my desk. From the other side of the office I notice Danny bounding towards me. His particular brand of mindless enthusiasm is the last thing I need right now, so I avoid eye contact and continue unpacking my bag. This does no good, however, as he makes his way over towards me, with all the gaiety of Tigger.

"Jesus dude," he says, slapping me heartily on the back, "what happened to you? You swim here or something?"

"*FUCK OFF!*" I snarl.

"Bloody hell mate," Danny says, taking a step back in shock, "no need for that, I was only having a laugh with you."

"I'm sorry Danny," I say, trying to swallow my rage. After all, it's not Danny's fault I'm feeling like this, just as I suppose it isn't his fault he's an idiot. "Don't take this personally, but I'm in a *really bad mood* today."

"Fair enough dude," he says backing away, making that hands-up, placating gesture people use, "I understand, we all have our bad days. I'll just keep out of your way today then."

I sincerely hope he does exactly that, as I think being called "dude" one more time may well drive me to murder and/or suicide.

The day fails to improve from this point. Each call is longer and more difficult than the last, and I am constantly aware of Richard watching me from his desk, or suspect that he is listening in to my every call, like a Stasi officer, waiting for me to make some sort of mistake. The hours drag by like never before, the hands of the clock on the office wall seeming to take forever to move that last minute until four o'clock. When that hour is finally reached, I make an instant decision to get drunk. I buy some cans and a bottle of whiskey on the way home, and spend the rest of the evening on the couch drinking them. I don't even switch on the TV. I just drink. When my phone rings I don't answer it. I just drink. I can't even be bothered to get in the shower. I just drink, and I keep on drinking until I feel my mood shifting from down-trodden lethargy to anger.

Fuck it. Fuck them all. Fuck my parents and their liberal views. Fuck their hypocrisy, lecturing their pupils on the evils of the slave trade while they get their wages paid into their high interest Barclay's bank accounts, a bank that was founded by a family who made their fortune from the fucking slave trade. Fuck them for ever conceiving me and fuck them for not aborting me, or at least drowning me at birth. Fuck my soulless, money-grabbing vampire of a brother in his mansion behind his security

132

gates. He'll be putting a fucking noose around his neck and hanging himself from the beam of his fucking wine cellar if the bottom ever falls out of the mobile phone industry, which I pray it does. I hope his investments fail and leave him fucking destitute. Fuck his bimbo wife, with her fake tits, fake tan and peroxide hair. Fuck their ugly, pampered little sprog with his piano lessons and private school, destined to grow into a carbon copy of my brother.

Fuck my friends too. Fuck Darren and Aimee and their childhood sweetheart bullshit romance. They had settled for each other before most people even start thinking about relationships, and staying together was probably just the easiest option. Fuck Jimmy and the degenerate queer lifestyle he has chosen to lead; sucking strangers' dicks in nightclub toilets in the middle of a worldwide AIDS crisis.

Fuck Brian and his tastefully furnished office, quietly passing judgement on me once a week. A man with a gut that fucking fat is in no position to judge anyone. Fuck him for forcing me into this stupid fucking job. Fuck him for indulging my self-absorption and solipsism. He's probably every bit as fucked up as me and the other fools who waste their money unburdening themselves with him every week.

Fuck Jenny and her arrogant pursuit of me. Can't that stupid fucking bitch take "no" for an answer? What the fuck does she think I am anyway? Presumably some sort of pet project for her. If she wants to save something, she should join Greenpeace and just leave me the fuck alone. If she's so fixated on someone like me there must be something severely fucking wrong with that girl.

Fuck this town. Fuck the smack-heads and the stinking, cider-drinking scum filling its streets. Fuck it's ugly town centre full of boarded-up shops. Fuck its disgusting pubs. Fuck the delis and mini-supermarkets being opened up all over it by immigrants from whichever backwards, war-ravaged, not-even-recognised-by-the-UN, eastern European, backwater state they come from. Fuck them for being stupid enough to want to live here, and fuck the small-minded idiots who target them for persecution. Fuck Birkenhead, fuck the Wirral, fuck Merseyside, fuck England and fuck Britain. Fuck the Union Jack, fuck its red, its white and its blue.

Fuck me too. Fuck Gary Lennon. Fuck my O.C.D. and my anxiety and my panic attacks. Fuck my squalid little flat and my ridiculous cleaning schedules and routines. Fuck me for letting myself become this sad, lonely little figure I am, as insignificant as piss in the rain. It's a lie to say that I don't blame anyone for the way I am. I blame myself. There is nobody else to blame. I've made myself into this pathetic waste of molecules, and it's too late now to do anything about it. Fuck every single aspect of my pointless, empty, directionless, wretched little life.

TWENTY-THREE

My eyes open slowly, gradually prising apart the crusty green sleep that glued them together. I'm still sitting on the couch, fully clothed. I think it is Tuesday morning. There is a dull ache in my guts which I haven't experienced before, and I wonder if this could be the first sign of stomach cancer. I stagger to the bathroom and look in the mirror. I look awful. Never exactly a beaming picture of health, today I look like fried shite. My face is covered in stubble, my eyes are blank and lifeless, the skin around them is red and puffy and, sticking out of the top of my head like some thin white gatecrasher, is a single grey hair. As I pluck it from my scalp I notice an intense feeling that I have barely experienced for a week now: hunger. *Ferocious* hunger. I glance at my clock and realise I've overslept so, knowing that I have insufficient time for a real breakfast before work, I stop at the shop on my way in and buy two sandwiches, crisps and a bottle of pop. Getting to my desk I put my lunch in my drawer, knowing that I will struggle to last the four hours until lunch to eat it. Time drags as I take call upon call. I'm so hungry now that I can hear my stomach growling. The voices on the other end of the phone are almost drowned out by the churning cacophony of noise emanating from my insides. The rumblings are so loud I have to raise my voice to hear myself above them. Co-workers turn to look at me as I almost yell at the customer down the phone. I notice Richard peep his pimply face from around his computer screen to look at me.

"There's no need to yell, I'm not deaf you know" says Mrs Hargreaves from Newton-le-Willows before she hangs up on me. Richard approaches me cautiously. I look at the clock and realise it's time for my morning coffee break. Before Richard can speak, I switch off my phone and jump out of my seat. As I do so he recoils slightly, as though expecting some sort of attack. Much as I would like to garrotte the ugly little shit with my phone wire, I am focussed on nothing other than getting out of there and eating before me and everyone else in the room is deafened by the rumblings of my stomach.

"Just gonna take my coffee break Richard," I say.

"Right, well, be back in ten minutes then," he says with a

vague look of suspicion and confusion.

"I've been working here for nearly a month now; I know exactly how long my coffee break is."

"Yeah well we've got a lot of calls queued so don't be late back," I think is the spotty bastard's reply, but I can't be certain over the din of my innards. I feel my fist clenching and every muscle in my body tighten as I fight the urge to punch his hideous little face out through the other side of his head. I open my drawer, grab my sandwiches and head towards the staff canteen. As I reach the door, I look back to see Richard still watching me. I feel a wave of self-loathing at not having jammed my thumbs into his eyeballs.

I sit in the first available chair in the canteen and tear open my sandwiches. It takes me less than a minute to devour them all, but I'm still nowhere near sated. I open my crisps and they are gone in seconds. What I'm feeling now is far beyond hunger. Suddenly I'm totally ravenous. I've never experienced a craving for food like this. I'm like a freshly arisen zombie on the hunt for brains. The starving millions in the most famine-hit parts of Africa have never been as hungry as I am right now. I sprint downstairs to the main entrance where every morning there is a woman dispensing sandwiches and various other snacks. I shoulder-barge my way to the front of the queue, ignoring the protests and insults, and grab a handful of them. I don't even care what I've grabbed, I just need more food. I throw a tenner at the woman and tell her to keep the change. For all I know a tenner doesn't cover the cost of what I've bought, but I don't wait to find out, and sprint back up the stairs to the canteen. As I sit back down I glance at the clock. I've got exactly three minutes before I have to be back at my desk. Three minutes to eat what turns out to be three more sandwiches, a chicken salad wrap, a bar of chocolate and a cream doughnut. I have no idea whether or not this will be time enough but I tear into them like a savage, ripping their plastic coverings off and grunting like some sort of animal as I gorge myself. I'd eat the packaging too, if only it were edible. I run over to the drinks machine with my mouth crammed full of food and bring back two more bottles of pop. As I shove the last bit of doughnut down my throat I open both bottles and down them in about ten seconds flat, before unleashing a monstrous belch. I look around, panting for breath

136

and see that everyone in the canteen is staring at me with absolute disgust. Some of them even move their arms to cover their own sandwiches, like school kids guarding an exam paper, no doubt fearful that I will wrestle their food from them in my quest for gratification. I look up at the clock and realise I should have been back at my desk a minute ago. I creep back into the main office. Richard has his head down, apparently engrossed in something, so I sign back onto my phone and hope I've got away with it. As soon as I'm settled though an internal call comes through. A look at my phone display panel confirms my suspicions by showing Richard's extension number. "Can you come over to my desk please Gary," he says as I answer, and hangs up before I can argue.

Richard still has his head down writing something as I walk over to his desk and sit down. When he looks up at me to speak he hesitates and stares at me. I look down and am mortified to see that my shirt is covered in bits of chicken, cheese and tuna mayo. Richard rolls his eyes slightly and begins to speak.

"What did I say to you before you went on your break?"

"I don't remember verbatim but I'm sure you're about to tell me."

A slight look of anger flashes across his face.

"I clearly told you not to be late back from your break. I told you we were very busy and had calls queued, and yet you still come back late."

"Come on Richard, it was less than a minute."

"Well if you thought that was acceptable, then why did you skulk back to your work station?"

"In the hope that I would avoid having to have a pointless little interaction such as this with you. Clearly though, I failed in that objective."

"I think you did it because you knew you were in the wrong and were trying to get away with it."

"Can I go back to my desk now? If there's so many fucking calls queued maybe you should let me go and answer some."

"In a minute, but first I'm going to have to give you a written warning."

"A written warning? For being one minute late back from my break? Do you realise that if I gave a flying fuck about this job I'd consider that grossly unfair?"

"You may not give a fuck about your job but I do about mine, and if your stats are bad then it makes me look bad. Just look at the state of yourself. You come in here every day as though you're doing us a favour by being here. There are plenty of people out there who'd be very grateful to have a job like yours. People who actually want to work. We're in the middle of a global recession. People are losing their jobs and their houses left, right and centre. People who've worked hard all their lives can't pay their bills, and you complain about having to come in here. You don't realise how lucky you are, but maybe this warning will give you the kick up the backside you need."

And with what in his sad little world is probably a motivational speech worthy of Lincoln, he begins to write out my warning.

I've had enough now. I've had enough of being talked down to by the kind of person who says "pacific" instead of "specific". I've had enough of being bullied by some fucking idiot who's actually three years younger than me. Once more I feel my fists clench and a tightening of every muscle and piece of sinew in my body. I can see the red mists descending in front of my eyes. I can feel entire oceans of rage boiling and bubbling up inside me. I begin some relaxation breathing, then decide that this time, I will not keep a lid on my anger. I look at the top of Richard's head as he writes out my warning and imagine what I could do to him. I could crumple up the disciplinary he's writing and shove it down his throat till he chokes. I could take the fountain pen from his hand and stab it so far into his eye that it penetrates his brain. I could pick up his computer monitor and smash it over his head. These would all be deeply fulfilling actions, but as I feel the mass of food churning around my stomach, I have an even better idea.

"You're a fucking amoeba," I say quietly. Richard looks up.

"What did you s—"

But before he can finish his sentence I'm on top of him. With one hand I tightly grip his tie and with the other I jam two fingers down my throat and vomit all over his face. As he screams I aim the streams of vomit directly into his mouth, and watch with delight as his screams cause my puke to bubble and gurgle inside his mouth. I straddle him on his chair and wrap my legs tightly round the back of it so there is no escape.

"Help! Help! For fuck's sake someone get him off me," he

138

manages to yell through a mouth full of my semi-digested food and stomach acid.

By the time anyone has managed to react, what seems like an endless stream of vile, stinking, bilious vomit has already covered the bastard, filling his eyes, mouth and nasal passages. I keep shoving my fingers down my throat until my guts are completely empty, and only bile and drool lands on his face. Eventually someone drags me off him, but I don't mind as the damage has been done. As I am pulled away Richard falls to the floor, sobbing like a fucking baby, making a pathetic attempt to blink the stinging sick out of his eyes. I stand up and turn around to see the entire office watching in disbelief. Some of the girls are crying, and men who tower above me step back away from me in sheer terror. Danny stares at me, agog.

"Fucking hell dude," he says.

I see the two security guards from downstairs running towards me from the far end of the office. I have just enough time to throw my phone and computer monitor to the floor before I am grabbed by the arms and dragged down the stairs towards the exit. Despite having no urge to resist I decide to go kicking and screaming anyway. As we reach the main door we pass the sandwich lady, who watches in horror.

"Thanks for the sandwiches," I say to her before I am hurled through the door and land face first on the pavement outside. I pick myself up and the security guards stare at me smugly from the other side of the thick glass door that separates us. I take a few steps back and run full force into the door, face first. As my face hits the glass I see their expressions change from smug to confused, then from confused to afraid as I do it again. The third time I do it my nose splatters blood all over the door, and by now the guards are clearly petrified. As one of them picks up the phone to call the police I decide it's time for me to leave.

I run home still covered in sick and with blood dripping from my nose. I run through the town centre and, when confronted by a thick crowd of shoppers, I put my head down and charge at them like a rampaging bull, and they part for me like the Red Seas parting for Moses. I give a pukey, bloody snarl to a bemused scally, grabbing the phone from his hand as I run past him, and silencing the terrible music coming from it by smashing it on the floor. A young man wearing an RSPCA anorak and carrying a clipboard takes an ill-advised step towards me, then withdraws as I scream a mouthful of vomit-smelling obscenities into his face. I keep running out of the shopping centre and up Oxton Road. As I turn onto my street, I pick up a brick and throw it through the window of the parked Mercedes. I get back to my flat and grab the bottle of whiskey from my kitchen cupboard and down the entire bottle in one fell swoop. As I pass out and fall towards the floor I think about what has just transpired, and think that at least things can't get any worse than this. Or so I thought. But the very next day, Buckle came back into my life.

TWENTY-FOUR

Jesus. Jesus fucking Christ. Buckle. He's back. The one person I neglect to include when quantifying the friends I have. The reason for this is, despite having known him longer than any of my other friends, sightings of him are so sporadic that I often forget he exists. How could I forget? How could anyone that has ever had any contact of any kind with him ever forget him?

To underline the impact his return is likely to have on my life, at this particular time, it is necessary for me to relay a few stories about him.

First, I should probably explain his slightly unusual nickname. His real name is Craig Macintyre, and we met when he arrived at my primary school when I was about six and straight away there was obviously something a little... different about him. My earliest recollection of him is during one playtime in the school yard. A small group of us were standing in a circle passing a football to each other. As one boy attempted to kick the ball to me, Craig appeared from nowhere, kicked the ball high over the school fence onto the busy road and ran off yelling "BUCKLE!! BUCKLE!!" (hence the nickname). Despite this bizarre incident, Craig and I quickly became quite friendly, mainly due to the fact that he'd moved into a house around the corner from me, and we would walk home together most days. It was during one such amble home that the next bizarre incident involving Craig occurred; one minute we were chatting away, the next minute Craig was nowhere to be seen. I looked around for a moment and eventually I saw, from the other side of the road, Craig's head protruding from the top of a Ford Capri with its convertible roof down. Assuming he was simply playing about in the car, I crossed over to him. I can still clearly recall the feeling of disgust and horror I felt when I discovered that, far from being engaged in some automotive role-play, he was squatted by the steering wheel with his pants down, depositing a huge shit directly into the centre of the driver's seat. I stood there in complete stunned silence, watching this enormous, coiled, snake-like turd accumulate on the seat of the car. I looked to the back of Craig's head as he slowly turned and looked me square in the eye. "BUCKLE!! BUCKLE!!" he yelled.

Now, while giving a little insight into the state of his mind, I realise these stories don't explain why it was such, or why he chose to shout that particular word at these moments. To be honest, I don't think any of us ever thought about it that much. Either that or we were too scared of him to ask. I found out the reason why during an after-school visit to his house one day.

We had been playing on Craig's Sega Master System when he accidentally knocked a drink over onto the floor. As he looked down at the glass of Ribena soaking into the white carpet he turned to me.

"Buckle! Buckle!" he yelled over and over. I panicked, thinking Craig's dad would hear from the next room, and think I was doing something terrible to his only child. When his dad came into the room though, I realised Craig wasn't talking to me, but was actually alerting his dad to what he had done.

"You fucking clumsy little rat. That carpet's fucking ruined now."

He lifted up his T-shirt to reveal a belt with a huge buckle in the shape of the Harley Davidson logo.

"Get in the front room," he said to Craig as he removed the belt. Craig furtively scuttled out of the room. His dad turned to me.

"Excuse us Gary," he said, and closed the door.

Through the walls I could hear the muffled sounds of the heavy buckle cracking against Craig's flesh, and a whimpered "Buckle" replaced the usual yell. I covered my ears so I didn't have to listen to it. A few minutes later Craig returned, sat back down beside me, and we continued playing Sonic the Hedgehog as though nothing had happened.

I never went to play at Craig's house much after that day.

The morning after my vomit escapades I wake up face down on the living room floor with an aggressive hangover, the stale stench of vomit-and-whiskey breath filling the room. It takes me a few minutes to remember the events of the previous afternoon, and then a few minutes more to convince myself that they did indeed happen and that I have not just had a particularly vivid and disturbing dream. I get into the shower wondering whether Richard could have me arrested. Does covering someone in vomit count as an assault? I am standing in my bathroom drying myself when my intercom sounds. My heart seems to stop for a moment and I approach the intercom nervously. I pick up the receiver and take a deep breath, expecting Her Majesty's Constabulary to be on the other end.

"Hello?" I say.

There is a pregnant pause before a familiar and blood-curdling voice emanates from the ear piece:

"BUCKLE!"

Oh sweet fucking Christ. It's been about three years since I last saw Craig, and almost as many since I even thought about him. The last I knew, he had joined the army, mainly because his volatile personality had prevented him from ever keeping a normal job for more than a few months. Personally, I was amazed that he was ever accepted into the armed forces. I always assumed that, before admitting someone, they would have to carry out some sort of psychological screening test, which Craig would surely fail. I was also terrified at the prospect of him being allowed near firearms and explosives, but I suppose they need to keep the numbers up, and there will always be a need for mindless killing machines or expendable cannon fodder to send into war zones. Then again, most people come out of the army deeply disturbed anyway, so I suppose Craig was just a few steps ahead of the rest of them.

I buzz Craig in and hear him bounding up the stairs to my flat.

"Waaaaaaaahhhhhaaaaaaaaaay" he says by way of a greeting as I open my front door to him. An eight pack of Tennant's Super Strength lager hangs from one hand, and an eight pack of Crest cider hangs from the other.

"Hello Craig," is the only response I can muster.

"Jesus. Don't sound so fucking enthusiastic, will ya?"

"Sorry, it's just... I wasn't expecting... aren't you... I thought you were with the army. Are you home on leave or something?"

"Ha ha, well you could say that mate." Craig sits down on my couch and begins to regale me with the story of how he came to be back in Birkenhead.

While he was stationed down in Aldershot, Craig was on a night out with "the lads". An evening of heavy drinking and the singing of highly offensive songs was followed by a visit to a local night club. Things were progressing very well when Craig pulled a local woman of questionable moral standards. After a period of sustained snogging and groping (or what Craig termed "getting me fingers a bit wet") in a dark corner of the club, the woman invited Craig to join her in her car outside. A few minutes later, in the car park opposite, the girl is, in Craig's slightly confusing words, "riding me like a fucking Grand National winner." But then, at the crucial moment, the car door is opened. Craig looks up to be confronted by the sight of one of the bouncers from the nightclub.

"What the fuck are you doing?" asks Craig indignantly.

"What the fuck am I doing?" repeats the bouncer. "What the fuck are you doing more like. That's my fucking missus you're shagging you little shit!"

And with that the adulterous woman is dragged off Craig's penis and thrown to the floor. Then Craig is dragged from the vehicle as the bouncer's meaty fists land punch after punch on his head and face. Craig attempts to run but, with his trousers around his ankles, struggles only a few steps and trips over. A vicious kick is administered to his guts as he lies prone on the ground. Considering Craig well and truly dealt with, the man turns his attentions to his errant spouse. Craig struggles to his feet and pulls his pants up as the bouncer delivers a full force slap across the face of his wife. Seeing a large piece of broken paving stone nearby by, Craig picks it up and approaches from behind. Just as he is about to slap the woman a second time, Craig brings the slab down on the back of his head with such force that it breaks in two. Rather than having the desired effect of knocking him out however, it merely stuns him. As he staggers around, Craig's barely concealed dark side takes over. He leaps on the bouncers back.

"BUCKLE!! BUCKLE!! BUCKLE!!"

As Craig tells his story, a vivid image of the scene forms in my head. A woman screaming, a huge ape of a man staggering around with blood pouring from his head, as a skinny Birkenhead psychopath rides him around like a knight on his trusty stead, yelling a surreal battle-cry. Unfortunately, I can also clearly visualise what is described to me next. Not content with this bizarre scenario, Craig reaches down and grabs the bouncer's nose. I can almost hear the horrific tearing of flesh as Craig describes to me how he literally ripped the man's nose from his face.

"My God, that's absolutely hideous," I say when the anecdote is thankfully over, "even by your standards Craig, that is truly hideous."

"Fuck him, fucking wife-beating piece of shit. But yeah, it was a bit mad like."

"A bit mad? Craig, you ripped off a man's nose. You actually ripped it off! What did you do with it?"

"I just chucked it away. I didn't need it did I? Then I stole a car to get away from there. Come to think of it, it was the bouncer's car."

"Oh great; so now we can add car theft to your recent list of crimes."

"Yeah I know man. So that's why I've had to come home. The police down there are probably looking for me."

"I don't think there's any probably about it. And what about the army? Will they be looking for you?"

"Well yeah they will be. That's the thing you see."

"What? What's the thing?" I ask, already knowing what is coming next.

"Well, they've obviously got my dad's address, not that I'd go there anyway, so I was wondering if it'd be OK to lie low here for a few days or so?"

"No! Absolutely not! Not a fucking chance. I'm sorry Craig but it's absolutely out of the question."

I've seen how this man lives. He would be a hideous, uncontrollable force of nature, bringing chaos into my carefully structured world, and the last thing I need is him staying here, leaving empty beer cans on the floor, wiping his arse on my towels and masturbating all over the place.

"Oh come on man, just for a few days. It'll be fun."

"No it won't, not for me. Look Craig I'd like to help you. I really would mate but, I just can't let you stay. You know I've got... certain... issues."

"You mean besides being a great big twat?" he asks in all seriousness.

"Yeah, you know what I'm talking about; it's just not good for me to have someone hanging around here. I need my space. I haven't had anyone in here for more than a couple of hours at a time since I moved in. You know what I'm like for being a bit of a loner?"

"Yeah?"

"And my thing about everything having its place? And my... routines and all that?"

"Yeah?"

"Well, that's become a bit more pronounced recently. I've got a very strictly ordered world here, and there's just no room for you inside that world. You can't begin to imagine the kind of disruption it would cause me to have someone else living here, even for a few nights. Even just for *one* night."

"Please Gary," he pleads with the most sorrowful look I've ever seen from a man who just relieved someone of their proboscis, "I've got nowhere else to go. If I can't stay here then I'm basically on the streets."

Even I can't refuse such pleas, and my resistance is worn down. I agree to let him stay, but tell him he can't use the spare room and will have to make do with the couch. I sink into my chair as Craig does an odd little celebratory dance around the living room.

"So how've you been anyway?" he asks when his excitement subsides. "You working at the minute or are you still dole scum?"

I tell him everything about my actions yesterday. Part of me feels a deep sense of shame at what I did. The other part of me is quite pleased that at least I didn't rip anyone's nose off. By the time I've finished my story, Craig is rolling around the floor in hysterics.

"Fucking hell man, that's the funniest fucking thing I've ever heard. That sounds like something I'd do." He sits back on the couch, rips off one of the cans of Tennant's and throws it to me. "I bet you could do with a drink," he says, still laughing.

"Craig, it's half past ten. In the morning," I say.

"Yeah I know. Cheers mate."

Several hours later, the cans have all been drunk, as have the second lot Craig went to the shop to buy. With no more beer, he's getting restless. "Let's go out!" he exclaims, rising up from the couch.

"Go out?" I ask. "Go out where?"

146

"I dunno, let's go downtown or something, hit a few pubs, maybe go to a club. Sample some of that fine Birkenhead cunt."

"I don't think that's a good idea. I really, really don't."

"Why the fuck not?"

"Well partly because the last time you went out drinking, a man lost his nose."

"Oh fuck off man," he says, genuinely offended, "it's not like I do that every time I go out."

"Well besides that, there's also the fact that people are likely to be looking for you. You know, the army, the police, whatever gangsters that bouncer happens to be affiliated with. I just think it would be advisable to exercise a little more discretion."

"Ahhh it'll be OK mate. I just fancy getting out for a bit and spraying a few female visages. No offence, but your flat isn't the most welcoming of environments. Come on, we'll just go for a few, and I'm buying."

I can think of few things worse than going downtown, with its succession of bars and pubs, each rougher and dirtier than the last. But on the other hand I know that at least it'll ensure Craig is out of my flat for a bit.

"Ok. We'll just go for a few," I say, knowing that there's a good chance that the night will end badly.

Downtown Birkenhead. The junction of Grange Road West, Oxton Road and Whetstone Lane. It's like the four fucking corners of hell. On one corner is a McDonald's, providing the staple diet of most of the townsfolk. Opposite there is Moodz Bar. This establishment opens at 9am every morning, and by 10am the pavement outside is full of toothless, pasty-faced men clutching half-drunk pints of cheap lager in one hand, and cigarettes smoked down to the filter in the other. Not much better is the Charing Cross, which likes to market itself as a "sports bar", which would probably be accurate, if people glassing each other could be considered a sport. Perhaps the worst of all though, is the Irish pub on the opposite corner. When I say Irish, the establishment is Irish in name only. I doubt anyone Irish has ever worked there, and the closest the patrons have ever got to Ireland is probably listening to a U2 album. This place has been closed down several times, due to a variety of drug, underage drinking and violence related infringements of the licensing laws, only to re-open a few weeks later under a different name. This time, it goes under the name O'Connell's. As well as all its other shortcomings, they also serve some of the worst Guinness I have ever tasted.

A few pints in I already feel like I'm hitting the wall. Craig, on the other hand, is in his element. I give up even trying to keep up with him as he downs pint after pint, frequently finishing off my drinks for me. The pub is filling up now with some pretty fearsome looking characters. The table nearest to us is full of beefy blokes, some of whom have clearly just finished working on a building site, the rest of whom appear to have been released from prison this very morning. Their presence makes me uncomfortable, but Craig is oblivious to it. I'm feeling pretty light-headed by this point, and I can actually feel myself beginning to nod off when Craig's voice drags me back to the land of the living.

"Christ, look at the fucking tits on that spunk receptacle."

I follow his gaze to a group of women who've just walked in. They are all scantily clad, despite the cold weather, and one in particular does indeed have the biggest pair of gravity-defying breasts imaginable.

"Bet you could poke your fucking eyes out on those nipples. I fucking love dirty scally slags like her. I'm having some of that," Craig says with a determined expression on his face, "wait here."

Before I can protest he's straight up to the busty wench. He taps her on the shoulder to get her attention. I can't hear what he's saying but it's clearly some quite devastating repartee, as he instantly has the woman in stitches. He beckons her closer and leans in to whisper something into her ear. Whatever he says this time certainly doesn't have the desired effect. As he's speaking I see the woman's face turn from amusement to shock and then, finally, to utter disgust. She pulls away from Craig, leans back, and then takes everyone by surprise by delivering a head-butt worthy of Yosser Hughes squarely onto Craig's nose. He falls backwards, crashing directly onto the table of builders and convicts, sending pints of lager and rank Guinness flying and smashing onto the floor. Luckily, before they can manage to converge on him, Craig is grabbed by the bouncers and thrown out of the pub. I follow closely behind as he is dragged through the door and dumped onto the floor outside. As the door is slammed shut on us, Craig turns to me.

"Can you believe the fucking injustice of this shit?"

The best response I can mange is a confused shrug of my shoulders. Craig picks up a discarded beer bottle and sends it crashing through the window of the pub.

"You fucking pair of cunts, I'm coming back here tomorrow night and I'm gonna fucking face-rape the pair of you," he yells. He stands there in defiance, no doubt eager to remove another bouncer's nose. I manage to drag him away before the doors re-open.

Minutes later we are stood in an alleyway as Craig pisses against a bin bag full of rubbish.

"Jesus, listen to the sound it makes when my piss hits the bin bag. Fucking amazing. Bet it sounds even better from inside the bag."

"Fucking hell," I yell at the back of his head, "why does everything with you have to descend into chaos? Is it impossible for you to avoid violent situations?"

"Come on, I wasn't the aggressor there. In case you've gone temporarily fucking blind, I never threw a single punch at anyone. And those bouncers were well out of line. I'd have been well in with those slags if it weren't for them."

"What? Are you fucking serious? One of them head-butted you in the face! I'd hardly describe that as being in with them."

"Yeah well it's still closer to a shag than you've had in a long time," he says zipping up his cock.

"Piss off."

"Oh I'm so sorry, have I offended you?" he says sarcastically. Then he grabs me around the waist. "Come here Gaz, I'll shag you even if no one else will." And he begins dry humping me against a nearby wheelie bin.

"Get the fuck off me you mad bastard," I protest.

"Shut up, you love it really you dirty little fucker. Come on; call me 'Buckle' bitch."

Just as Craig says this, I see three scallies enter the alleyway in the corner of my eye.

"Look at this fucking pair of dirty queers," one of them says to his mates.

Far from the denials he was no doubt expecting, what he instead gets is Craig squaring up to him and grabbing his crotch through his tracksuit trousers.

"Yeah I'm fucking queer, fancy a fuck or what?"

"Eeeew you dirty faggot," says the scally, pushing Craig away. The three of them begin to advance on us. We're cornered in the alleyway, but Craig leaps athletically onto the wheelie bin and holds both arms aloft.

"I am Chingachgook, the last of the Mohicans," he yells portentously. "Do *NOT* fuck with me!" And with that he kicks the first scally in the face, before leaping majestically over the other two and running out of the alley, round the corner and out of sight. Knowing they have no chance of catching him, the scallies decide to administer a beating to me alone. I hold up my hands in a peaceful gesture as they advance on me.

"Listen lads – " is all I am able to say before I am head-butted in the face. A clumsy but very painful punch to the side of the head quickly follows, knocking me against the wheelie bin. The knee into my bollocks is what puts me on the ground. I try to get back up but am kicked in the face. After I feel another foot in my kidneys, I instinctively curl up into a ball.

As the kicks and punches rain down on my head and torso, I hear the distant cry.

"BUCKLE!"

When I finally manage to stagger home, blood dripping from my nose and with several cuts to my face, I find Craig sitting outside my flat on the chair that once resided in the corner of my living room, rolling himself a cigarette and laughing at me.

"You never were much of a fighter."

I realise that every minute spent with this man moves me a minute closer to my doom.

"It's a stony path down which you lead me," I say, wiping some blood from my face. He looks at me quizzically.

"You always talked a lot of shit too."

TWENTY-FIVE

I am awoken early the next morning by a text message on my mobile, which turns out to be from Jimmy. I compose a brief text reply, but my message fails to send with every attempt. I walk through to the living room and wake Craig up.

"Have you been using my mobile?" I ask him. He starts laughing to himself. "What? What's so funny?"

Craig sits up and wipes some sleep from his eyes.

"I'd forgotten about that."

"What had you forgotten about? Where has all my credit gone? What the fuck have you done this time?" Craig starts laughing again.

"Well," he says as he adjusts the morning wood in his boxer shorts, "I was a bit bored when we got in last night, so I took your phone into the bog with me..."

"Oh Christ, Craig. What did you do?"

"...I just used your phone to film myself having a piss, then I sent the video off to a few people."

"You fucking what? I had nearly five pounds' worth of credit on there. That usually lasts me at least a month. Who the hell did you send it to, exactly?"

"Nobody in particular. Just a load of random numbers."

"You mean you didn't even know them? So dozens of complete strangers are currently receiving a video of you urinating into my toilet?"

"Yeah," Craig says as though this is perfectly normal, "a nice big fucking frothy piss it was too. Top quality. Which is more than I can say for the video itself. The camera on your phone is fucking shit mate. You need to upgrade."

"The quality of the camera on my phone really is not the issue here, the issue is you using that camera to film yourself pissing, and then using all my credit to send the video to a bunch of complete strangers. You'll probably get me arrested or something, as well as wasting my money. Fucking hell Craig, you're an animal."

Craig shrugs his shoulders, as though I'm being completely unreasonable.

"Just having a laugh mate," he says.

Craig gets dressed and we walk up to the shop. As I have been pissing blood this morning and have several highly visible bruises and ache all over from the beating I received last night, I have no desire to leave my flat, but Craig has a huge craving for some pickled onion Monster Munch, and insists that I join him. He pays for a handful of packets of his desired snack, and waits in the corner by the door as I shuffle around the shop, picking a few essentials. I'm walking towards the counter when the hulking figure of my shop nemesis strides through the door, talking loudly on his mobile phone. Naturally, as I'm next in line to be served, he steps in front of me, taking a second to glance at my bruises and laughing to himself. Craig has witnessed this from his corner of the shop and is clearly incensed.

"Aye aye!" he shouts, but the Neanderthal is too engrossed in his mobile conversation to notice. Not wanting to receive another beating, I gesture to Craig to desist from this course of action, but he's not interested.

"Oi, bollocks," he shouts even louder. Just in case he hasn't made himself heard, he launches one of his packets of Monster Munch violently at the side of The Thing's head. By now, a queue has formed behind me, and they are all engrossed in this developing situation. The Thing stops talking on his phone, looks down confusedly at the corn snack missile he's just been hit with, and turns around to face Craig.

"What the fuck are you doing?" he asks, not unreasonably.

"I might ask you the same fucking question. Didn't your mother teach you any fucking manners? Or was she too busy getting gang-fucked by the kind of orang-utans that presumably impregnated her with you, you fucking meatheaded twat?"

I hear some of the people behind me snickering, but I'm far too scared to share their amusement.

"Who the fuck do you think you're talking to?" asks The Thing.

"The biggest, ugliest, most ignorant, kebab-handed fucking cunt I've ever fucking seen." The Thing tries to speak, but Craig cuts him off. "You could see there was someone about to get served, but you just pushed your way to the front of the queue. You obviously think that being a big fuck-ugly baboon gives you the right to treat people like shit, but I don't give a fuck how big you are, or how many fucking steroids you had for breakfast, I still expect basic fucking courtesy. Now get to the fucking back of that fucking queue, or I'll come over there, and I'll take that poncey fucking phone from your gristly fucking hand and insert it right into your fucking Jap's Eye. But first, you're gonna apologise to the man behind you, and you're gonna fucking mean it."

The Thing turns to look at me. I can't believe Craig has dragged me into this. Not content with getting me beaten up in an alleyway, he now wants to get me killed in a convenience store. I'm trembling so much I can barely hold my milk and loaf of bread. I'm certain I'm going to be smashed into the ground, at which I suspect Craig would simply laugh and walk away.

"Sorry," grunts The Thing , and he skulks to the back of the queue.

I'm stunned. The biggest, meanest-looking bastard I've ever seen is actually apologising to me. In public. In front of a load of strangers. And it's all thanks to Craig. I've never had a hero in my life before today, but for a moment I do. And it's an unhinged, Monster Munch-eating man who chooses to call himself Buckle.

153

TWENTY-SIX

I'm standing in a large, expensively decorated room. All around me are wealthy, handsome and intelligent-looking people. I stare at them, and they all stare back at me. But they are not looking at me with contempt, disgust or any of the negative motivations with which people usually look at me. In fact, they are all smiling at me, and appear transfixed by me.

"Please continue Mr Lennon," one of them says, "we do so enjoy your anecdotes." So I start talking. I have no idea what I am saying, to me it sounds like unintelligible gibberish. However, to my audience it is clearly the most devastatingly witty banter they have ever heard. I still cannot decipher a single word I'm saying but, judging by the reactions of the assembled crowd, I am by turns funny, insightful, and thought-provoking. Each garbled noise that falls from my mouth induces laughter, tears or respectful silence.

"Oh Mr Lennon, you truly are quite the raconteur," says another of my devotees. It appears that I am Noel Coward, JFK and Jesus all rolled into one.

Then it all starts to go wrong. While I'm mid-sentence, a cloud forms before us, from which none other than Craig emerges. He's wearing an expensive-looking tuxedo, the white shirt of which is flecked with spots of blood. He leans in very close to me and whispers softly.

"Buckle."

"Craig," I say, steering him away from my new crowd of admirers, "where did all that blood come from? What have you done?"

"There was some cunt over there slagging off Stravinski's 'The Rite of Spring', so I told him that it was one of the most innovative pieces of music of the 20th century, and that its polytonalities have yet to be surpassed. Then I glassed the fucker in the face."

I hear a flurry of activity behind Craig, and look over his shoulder to see a man with a jagged shard of glass sticking out of his face, being tended to by other guests. I look back to Craig, who is now standing on a table with his trousers pulled down to his knees, wanking thick dollops of dark brown semen into the punch bowl. The woman who just moments earlier was enraptured by my every word turns to me with a look of horror.

"Mr Lennon, how could you bring this uncouth ruffian into our midst?"

I try to apologise but, once again, the words that come out of my mouth are completely incomprehensible. But instead of provoking laughter and reverence, this time they provoke only looks of disgust. Some people cover their ears to block out the hideousness of whatever it is I'm saying. One woman actually faints in horror, hitting her head on the corner of an ice sculpture as she falls. Blood spurts out of the gaping wound on her head, colouring the pristine white table cloth a hideous shade of red. Suddenly the crowd turns on me, and begins to stampede towards me with pitchforks and burning torches in their hands, and a collective blood lust in their eyes. I turn and run, but Craig doesn't run with me. Instead he turns to the crowd, suddenly dressed not in a tuxedo, but as some sort of ancient Celtic warrior, covered in mud and shit and holding aloft a fearsome looking Shillelagh.

"BUCKLE," he yells, and runs towards them, swinging his weapon wildly above his head, smashing the skulls of any party-goer in his path. I turn to run in the opposite direction but Richard is standing before me, blocking my path.

"Richard, what the fuck are you doing here?" I ask.

"I'm not Richard anymore," he answers in monotone.

"Who are you then?"

"I am the Puke Monster."

"How did you become the Puke Monster?" I ask.

"You turned me into the Puke Monster, Gary. And you ruined my favourite tie."

"You're no puke monster, you're just some titty biscuit who works in a call centre," I say mockingly. Richard looks offended.

"Can a titty biscuit do this?" he asks, as thick, streaming jets of projectile vomit begin to spray out of his mouth, his eyes, his nostrils. Every single orifice in his head gushes forth with the stuff, every last bit of it arching directly towards my face.

My intercom buzzes. I wake up slightly panicked. It's been a few days since I evacuated my guts over Richard, but there's still a good chance the police could become involved. I get out of bed, throw some clothes on and go to the intercom. As I do I hear the TV playing in the living room. I turn and see Craig sitting on the couch in his boxer shorts eating cornflakes out of a large pan. In the corner I think I can hear *Jeremy Kyle* on TV. I lift up the intercom receiver and prepare myself for the worst.

"Hello?"

"Gary?" asks a female voice I don't recognise straight away.

"Yes? Who is it?"

"It's me."

"Jenny? Is that you?"

"Yeah it is. Look Gary, I'm really sorry to call round like this but I was worried about you. I heard about what happened the other day and I suppose I just wanted to see if you were alright. It's all anyone in work has been talking about. I wanted to hear from you what actually happened. You know, give you the chance to give your side of the story. The stuff I've been hearing in work, it was just too – "

"Believe me," I interrupt, "whatever you've heard couldn't possibly be any worse than what actually happened."

"Oh. Right. Shit. How are you?"

"Erm... yeah, I'm OK. I... how did you find out where I live?"

"I got Paul in HR to give me your address, I hope you don't mind."

"No I suppose not," – in fact I actually find this to be a huge intrusion, and I can't stop myself from wondering what she had to offer Paul in order to obtain my address. For a split-second my mind is filled with an image of Jenny on her knees, Paul from HR's cock buried deep in her throat. I shake my head to dislodge the thought – "that's quite enterprising. So, how's Richard? Has anything been said? I've been expecting the police to kick down my door anytime now."

"Well Richard's taken a few days off. To be honest I think he's too embarrassed to call the police or anything like that so I think you're off the hook there. Gary, I don't want to intrude, but would it be alright if I came in? Just for a bit of a chat?"

I look around at my once-spotless flat, and the detritus that now engulfs it. I think of the bruises on my face and how they must look. I look over to my couch at Craig; pan of cereal in hand, empty beer cans scattered around his feet, left bollock hanging unashamedly out of the side of his boxer shorts, vast morning wood straining to be free.

"It's not really a good time Jenny. Sorry."

"No that's fine, I understand. I'm gonna go now Gary, but I'm gonna leave a bit of paper with my mobile number on it. If you want to talk to me, or go for a drink or anything, just give me a ring. OK?"

"Yeah OK, I will do soon. Thanks Jenny."

"Bye Gary."

And with a click of the intercom she's gone.

"Who was that?" Craig enquires.

"Just a girl from work. Well, from where I used to work anyway."

"A girl? Calling for you? Fuck me mate, let's have a look at her."

He jumps up from the couch and runs to the window.

"Craig don't," I protest, "just leave it." But he's already at the window.

"Phwoooar, look at the fucking arse on her. I'd like to suck her intestines out through her fucking sphincter."

"Leave it Craig."

"I'd fuck ten different shades of shit out of that. What the fuck does a sexy little fuck pig like that see in a fucking weirdo like you?"

"Craig, that's enough."

"I'd fuck her so hard I'd impregnate her entire family. Tell you what mate, if you're not interested, tell her to come and see old Buckle if she wants her arse ploughing into the ground!"

I run over to Craig and drag him away from the window by his ears, and turn him around to face me.

"*SHUT THE FUCK UP!*" I yell into his face, bits of spit flying in every direction. "*DON'T YOU EVER FUCKING TALK ABOUT HER LIKE THAT YOU FILTHY DEGENERATE FUCKING SAVAGE. SHOW SOME FUCKING RESPECT. IF I EVER HEAR YOU TALKING ABOUT HER LIKE THAT AGAIN I'LL FUCKING STRANGLE YOU.*"

Craig stares at me with all the disbelief of a child who has just been slapped in the face by Santa Claus.

"Jesus Gaz, I'm sorry man, I didn't mean anything by it."

"Didn't mean anything by it? You talk like a fucking serial

rapist. You make me fucking sick. And just look at the fucking state of this place," I kick the pile of empty cans at him, "you're a fucking slob. I had this place just how I wanted it until you came here, now it's worse than a fucking pigsty. Now I want this place cleaned, and cleaned properly. If it's not done in an hour you can find some other poor bastard whose life you can turn upside down."

"OK Gaz, I'm sorry man, I'll do it – " But I'm not listening, I run down the stairs and find the piece of paper with Jenny's number on. I put it in my pocket and run back to my flat and get back into bed.

After a few more hours sleep, I emerge to see that Craig has made an effort at cleaning my flat. It's not clean by my standards, but, considering the closest he's ever got to house cleaning is blasting encrusted bits of shit off the toilet bowl with his own piss, it's a decent effort, and he manages to persuade me, against my better judgement, to allow him to take me for a drink by way of an apology. Tonight he seems in a comparatively restrained mood. He drinks like a fish as usual, but thankfully the pub is fairly quiet, so the potential for his regular tumult is significantly lessened. In fact, he seems almost contemplative.

"Can I ask you something Gaz?"

"I suppose so."

"Why do you never call me Buckle?"

"Because it's a ridiculous moniker. Your name is Craig Macintyre, which is a perfectly good name. If you insist on having a nickname, then surely something like 'Macca' would be more apt."

"Yeah but everyone has a name like that. Everyone calls me Buckle."

"But not everyone knows why you call yourself that. If they knew the reason why then I doubt everyone would use it. People probably think it's just something you made up as a kid and they think it's funny, but the motivation behind you saying it is far from fucking funny. I'll never forget that day round at yours."

As I'm speaking Craig's eyes have begun to wander and he's blatantly losing interest in what I'm saying. I assume a woman with big tits has passed through his line of vision.

"Craig, are you even listening to me?" He obviously isn't.

158

"Well fuck me in the nasal passages," he says, still looking past me, "what fresh hell is this? The fucking haircuts have landed."

I turn around to decipher what my psychotic friend is talking about now. It appears that he is referring to a bunch of young lads who have taken a table near to ours. They are all about twenty, and do indeed all have some of the most ridiculous haircuts I have ever seen. They've all gone for the quasi-mullet style cut that is seemingly in vogue with every young man in the country at the moment. They look as though someone has slashed wildly at their hair with a machete, resulting in all manner of angular pointed fringes, eyes half covered with oblique plumage and jagged, intersecting tufts jutting out at seemingly random places.

"What the frig is the story with those haircuts lads? Are you the latest X-Factor rejects boy-band or something?"

His voice has become about 50% louder so that not only the haircuts can hear him, but also every one else in the pub can hear them being mocked. I turn slightly in my chair to gauge their reaction. None of them speaks up. Instead they shift uncomfortably in their seats and attempt to ignore their castigator. Normally I am the first person to condemn people like them. They look ludicrous and are all probably idiots, but for some reason I can't stop myself feeling some measure of pity for them. I'm not certain anyone truly deserves to be on the receiving end of a heckling from "Buckle", and their apparent inability to defend themselves seems truly pathetic to me. I find myself imagining how I would feel in their predicament, and I know that I too would be as impotent as they currently are. I suppose this is what most people would recognise as empathy.

"Leave it Craig," I say quietly.

"What do you mean leave it?" he asks.

"I mean, just leave them alone, you've had a laugh but just leave it now, they're just trying to have a drink, it's not like they're doing you any harm or anything is it?"

Craig looks at me with complete disgust.

"What the *fuck's* got into you?"

"Nothing's got into me," I say in my best diplomatic voice, "I just think you shouldn't take the piss out of people like that. They're just minding their own business and you're shouting abuse at them. There's no need for it."

"Fucking hell mate, what are you, the voice of fucking reason all of a sudden? Excuse me for fucking breathing, only I thought I'd come for a drink with my mate Gary Lennon, but it looks like I've actually ended up with Koffi Fucking Annan! Since when do you defend fucknuts like that lot?"

As he says "fucknuts", he intentionally raises his voice again to make sure they have definitely heard him, and also gestures towards them to leave them in absolutely no doubt that it is them he is referring to.

"Stop it," I say. "It's not a case of defending them, it's just... I just would like to spend an evening where you don't end up beating someone up, or getting beaten up yourself."

"Me get beaten up? By fucking One Direction over there?" He laughs heartily at this highly unlikely scenario.

"Not so much that, just... you always have to throw yourself into these volatile situations, and if there isn't a volatile situation to throw yourself into, then you have to create one. Like that time when you started a fight with that pair of builders just because they were listening to Fleetwood Mac while they worked."

"I won the fucking fight didn't I? Fuck them anyway, fucking pair of racists."

"How do you know they were racists?"

"Well they were reading *The Sun*, so they were at least cunts. Fuck them and Rupert Murdoch. And in my defence, I was off my tits on glue."

"In your defence? The fact that you had spent the day in a wheelie bin inhaling a bunch of potent solvents is not a mitigating factor. We were fourteen years old. Christ, just days ago you ripped the nose from a man's face, and now you're basically a fugitive. I just wish you'd show a little more discretion. The very least you might end up doing is getting yourself caught, and at worst, one day you might just get yourself into a situation that you can't control, and you could end up getting yourself killed."

Craig puts down his pint and leans in towards me slightly, looking genuinely moved by what I've said.

"Why Gary Lennon, you big soft cunt," he says gently, "you actually fucking care about me. I didn't think you gave a flying fuck about anyone, but you actually fucking care about me."

He leans back and downs the last of his pint.

"You don't have to worry about me Gaz," he continues, "I'm fucking bulletproof mate."

We finish our drinks and I manage to convince Craig that we should call it a night, no doubt much to the relief of the haircuts. Before we go back to my flat, though, Craig is adamant that we should go for a long walk. I decide that, even for Craig, there is little opportunity to cause trouble when just going for a walk, so I agree. Nearly an hour later we are still walking. Craig has kept me talking so much that I don't realise the distance we have travelled. I have no idea where we are as we turn up a quiet but familiar looking residential street. About two thirds of the way up, Craig stops outside a small terraced house and I realise, to my horror, where we are.

"Dad!" Craig shouts. "Are you in there you old bastard?"

"Fucking hell Craig," I say, "what the fuck are we doing here?"

"Oh nothing much," he replies, still shouting as loud as he can, "just thought I'd stop by and say hello to the Pater Famalias. Come on Dad, aren't you going to invite us in for a cup of tea?"

I see a curtain twitching on the first floor of the house, and Craig has apparently seen it too.

"Ah, there you are you brutal old fucker. It's me, your only child, come home to roost. Why don't you come down and open the door and we'll have a nice father-son chat about old times."

Lights are starting to come on in other houses now, and I grab Craig by the arm. "Come on Craig, let's head back to mine now, before someone calls the police or something."

He pulls his arm away from my grip.

"Yeah maybe you're right Gaz. I can always come back and see you some other time, can't I Daddy? I could pay you a visit any old time, day or night. One thing before I go though."

He walks up the path to the front door of the house where he grew up, pulls down his trousers, opens the letter box and presses his arse against it.

"Fucking hell Craig, what the fuck are you doing now?"

But Craig doesn't answer. The only thing breaking the silence is the soft thudding sound of the perfectly aimed, and presumably gargantuan, shit hitting the carpet inside. Craig leans back and looks up at the window.

"Special delivery," he shouts.

We make the long walk back to my flat. I head straight to my bedroom and leave Craig drinking and listening to music in the living room. My bedroom is where I now spend most of my time. Since Craig moved himself in it has become almost impossible for me to maintain my regular cleaning routines. I have tried several times to tidy to my usual specifications, but Craig is either in the way or, just as I have cleaned one section of a room, he has already dirtied or disarranged it by the time I get to the end of the next section. It's like trying to perform housework in the middle of a hurricane, and has proven to be completely futile. I have decided, therefore, that during Craig's stay with me, I had might as well write off the majority of my flat, as I am clearly unable to protect it from the wave of destruction Craig brings with him. It pains me to see my home in such a sorry state, and to compensate for this I have become even more fastidious in my bedroom. I have taken to cleaning it thoroughly every morning and every night before bed, and have developed a separate system for cleaning it for each time of day. In many ways I have become a prisoner in my own home, but I can currently see no other solution to what I hope is a temporary situation. Having left Craig in the living room, I perform my nightly cleaning ritual. Along with the beer I have consumed, this tires me out sufficiently that when I finally go to bed an hour or so later, I manage to fall asleep almost instantly.

I awake with a jolt a few hours later when my bedroom door is suddenly kicked in. I sit up in bed, and look towards the door. As my eyes adjust to the light coming in from the hall, I realise Craig is standing in my bedroom doorway. Against the light he is half silhouetted, but I realise he is holding an almost empty bottle of vodka, wearing just a T-shirt and a hefty pair of hiking boots.

"What the fuck are you doing Craig?" I wait several seconds for him to speak, but he just stands there looking at me. I pull the duvet right up to my chin, wondering if I am in any danger. I focus on the boots.

"Are they my old walking boots?" I ask.

Craig doesn't answer. Instead he turns and walks slowly back towards the living room. I hear some rustling, followed by a

162

single almighty bang. A few seconds of silence follows, then "She Drives Me Crazy" by the Fine Young Cannibals blasts from the stereo. I know for certain that I do not possess this song in my record collection, and Craig brought no CDs with him when he came, so I have no idea where he has managed to find it. I get up and close my door, dragging my chest of drawers across it to prevent any further encroachment. I shove some bits of tissue into my ears and try to get back to sleep.

I sleep well into the afternoon, something I haven't done for a long time. The only reason I wake up is because I can't sleep through the constant banging of cupboards and annoyed mumbling coming from my kitchen. I want to stay in bed, but I know I will never get any peace until whatever the problem Craig is having is resolved, so I reluctantly drag myself from my bed and walk through to the kitchen where, sure enough, Craig is searching frantically through each cupboard.

"I see you've finally decided to grace me with your fucking presence then," he says without removing his head from the cupboard it's buried in, "not exactly the host with the fucking most are you?"

"What exactly are you looking for?" I ask impatiently.

"What the fuck do you think I'm looking for?" Craig asks, at last taking his head out of the cupboard and turning to face me. "I'm looking for some fucking food. There's never any fucking food in this flat. What's wrong with you? Don't you fucking eat or something?"

"Of course I eat," I say, "it's just that I only ever buy enough for two or three days at a time." Craig looks at me as though I've just told him I grow my own food in a sock I keep hanging in my cupboard.

"Well that's a bit fucking stupid isn't it? Why don't you just go to the supermarket and buy in bulk you numpty?"

"Because I loathe supermarkets." Craig rolls his eyes.

"And exactly why do you hate supermarkets Gary? Please tell me because I'm just fucking dying to know and I can see you're just dying to tell me."

I know full well he's being sarcastic, but seeing as he's asked, I'm going to tell him.

"Because, I find them deeply depressing. Everything about

163

them. The way they have those rows and rows of trolleys lined up at the entrance, like hospital gurneys or something. And then when you step inside, they have those little automatic gates with arrows actually telling you which way to walk. They've obviously assumed that their customers are all so fucking stupid that they actually need to be told which direction to walk in. Mind you, their customers have probably been turned into such zombies from all the chemicals in and on their food that they probably *do* need to be told where to walk. I don't buy most of my food from the organic veg shop because I'm some sort of hippy, I just don't want to be poisoned by pesticides and preservatives every time I bite into a piece of broccoli. And at least when I go to the market or the veg shop I don't have to worry about getting caught up in the midst of huge crowds of people bashing each other out of the way with those trolleys. They use them like fucking dodgem cars sometimes, it's actually genuinely frightening. The old people are the worst; they've just got no regard for the safety of others. And then there's the staff they employ. Half of them look like they're on the verge of having some sort of learning disability, and the other half give those false fucking smiles and false polite chit-chat that you know they've been trained to say. Then you have some obnoxious teenager representing some local sports club or charity packing your shopping, extremely badly at that, and expecting you to make a fucking financial contribution to their club for the privilege. After going through all that you then have to get past the *Big Issue* sellers standing outside. The whole experience is a fucking nightmare, I'll stick with the smaller shops thank you very much."

Craig stands up and closes the cupboard door.

"You really are one fucked-up little man aren't you? You do realise that while you're having these sad little thoughts and trying to be a clever fucking twat, some people are actually busy living real lives? And you're forgetting the one great thing about supermarkets Gaz."

"And what might that be?"

"They're a fucking good place to pull?"

"What? Pull? As in pull a woman? For sex?"

"Fuck yeah! You wouldn't understand this, seeing as you haven't had sex since 1853, but supermarkets are full of

164

housewives. Housewives who are bored with their husbands, and are absolutely gagging for a good fucking seeing to from a well-hung young cock-slinger like me. Believe me Gaz, I've had more middle-aged fanny in supermarkets than I have at all the grab-a-granny nights I've ever been to. And I've been to a fuck load of grab-a-granny nights."

"Craig, is it possible for you to spend a minute in public without trying to shag someone? I mean, do you see every time you step outside the door as just another opportunity to stick your penis in something?"

Craig mulls this over for a second.

"Pretty much, yeah. Anyway," he says walking towards the front door, "you can starve as much as you want but I'm going the fucking chippy."

Craig slams the door behind him, then quickly re-opens it and sticks his head back in.

"Lend us a fiver to go the chippy?"

For most people, going to the chippy takes a few minutes, but I don't see Craig again all evening. I make a superficial attempt at cleaning up, drink a couple of beers and go to bed, wondering whether Craig has finally managed to get himself caught, or entwined in some ungodly set of circumstances, and consider the possibility that maybe he has simply moved on. His bag is still here, but the scant belongings he brought with him could easily be left behind. Perhaps I'm free.

My hopes are soon dashed when I hear Craig coming in. Much worse though, is hearing voices in the hallway. He's brought someone back with him. A woman. Instead of heading straight into the living room, Craig knocks on my bedroom door, and pokes his head around the door.

"Gaz, you awake mate?"

"Well if I wasn't before, then I certainly am now aren't I?"

"Good, I'm glad you're still up. Listen mate, I've got someone with me."

"I know you've got someone with you. How could I not know? Your voice has only two settings; loud and very loud. And your latest sexual conquest isn't much subtler."

Craig holds his head in his hands as he walks over and sits on the edge of my bed.

"Fucking hell Gaz, you've got a brain like a fucking prison riot. There's shit flying everywhere. Give it a rest."

"Don't tell me to give it a rest Craig. I've got every fucking right. When I reluctantly agreed to let you stay in my flat, I accepted that you would make a mess of the place. I accepted you would take money off me to get drunk with. I even accepted that you would end up getting me beaten senseless in a fucking alleyway. What I didn't accept, what I absolutely *will not* accept is you bringing some fucking slag back here to fuck on my couch. When you finally leave here, I want to be able to get this place back to normal, which will be very difficult if I have to look at your spunk stains every time I go to sit down. Who the hell is she anyway?"

"I don't know her name or anything. She's just some prozzie I met."

For a moment I think I must be having another vivid dream. Just minutes ago, I thought Craig might have inflicted his final indignity upon me, now he drags me down to this level of vicarious depravity.

"A what?!? A fucking prostitute? Jesus fucking Christ Craig. As if all the other stuff wasn't bad enough, you now bring some pox-ridden whore into my home? Well no way, you're not shagging her here."

"Gaz, that's what I've been trying to tell you, if you'd just shut your fucking word hole for a minute. I haven't brought her back here for me to shag, I've brought her back for you."

This is an unexpected development.

"What? Why would you do that?"

"It's a little present. Just my way of saying thanks. You know, for letting me stay here and everything."

"Craig, most people would have just bought a card or something, not some rancid hooker."

"That's it though, she's not rancid. Listen, I met her down by the park. This is her first night as a prozzie. Or so she says anyway. She's young, she's not bad looking, and she seems really clean. That's why I thought you'd be into her, I mean, I know how into cleanliness and hygiene you are."

"Well that's very considerate of you."

"My pleasure mate," he says as he gives me a friendly punch on the arm, my sarcasm clearly not registering. "Oh, you'll

166

obviously have to pay for her yourself like, you know, with me being a bit skint and that."

"Craig, I realise that within the context of your debauched mind this is probably a lovely gesture, but please, tell her to leave. I really don't need a prostitute."

Craig laughs as though this is the funniest thing he has heard in a long time.

"Gaz, mate, trust me; if anyone, anywhere needs a fucking prostitute, then it's you. You are without doubt the most uptight person I've ever met. Seriously Gaz, I'm not just taking the piss out of you now, I'm really not, but you need to get laid. Nobody can go as long without sex as you have without going completely fucking insane. You need this mate, it'll be good for you. And you haven't had any in such a long time you'll probably shoot your load in about five fucking seconds anyway, so it'll be over before you know it, and it might make you into a bit less of a twat. And if she's any good, maybe we can go twos-up on her. Although I suppose you wouldn't be into the idea of our balls touching and stuff. But there's no harm in you doing her."

His choice of words is crass, and his tone insulting, but maybe Craig has a point. Maybe paying for sex could provide some sort of solution for me. I have never had any moral objection to prostitution, and as I've always said, my avoidance of sex isn't caused by not actually liking it. It's caused by a dislike of what comes with it. Having regular sex with someone usually means getting into a relationship, which I have no interest in, and to be able to obtain casual sex, one would need to be skilled and confident with the opposite sex, but my lack of skill with people in general is even more pronounced where women are concerned. The only issue that would stop me from engaging in the act would be the obvious concerns about hygiene and disease. But Craig seems to have thought of everything, if this woman is indeed as clean as he states.

"Come on Gaz," he says, perhaps sensing the lessening of my resistance, "at least have a look at her. What harm can it do?"

Reluctantly, I nod my consent. Craig scurries out of the room, and returns seconds later with the prostitute. He was right; she is quite young; probably no older than twenty, so the drug addiction or desperate poverty that has presumably driven her to prostitution has not yet had time to completely ravage her looks.

She appears pretty clean. Perhaps not to my standards, but if I were to go through with this, I could ask her to take a bath or a shower first. But where would I do it? Even if I did decide to have sex with this woman, I wouldn't want her in my bed. Even a clean stranger would leave dead skill cells all over it, and I don't think any amount of washing would totally rid the sheets of the inevitable sullying the act would bring. I wouldn't want to do it on the couch for the same reason. Suddenly the arguments in favour of this sordid little proposal of Craig's are vastly outweighed by those against. I take another look at the whore, and am disgusted with myself for even contemplating it.

"So, what do you think?" Craig asks.

"Get her the fuck out of my flat," I say.

TWENTY-SEVEN

I turn the shower temperature control up high. I do the same with the pressure control, and keep going until they hit maximum, and the bathroom fills with steam. I love a good, hot and powerful shower. The hotter and stronger the better. When I get in the shower, I want to feel like it's almost burning and blasting a layer of skin off. Now *that* would be clean. In fact, it would probably be the only way to be truly clean. No matter how much you shower, there is probably always something on your skin that escapes it, even if it's just the smallest microbe. But if you actually took a layer of skin off, well, nothing is going to survive that. I've been having this particular shower for almost an hour, and I don't think I'll be getting out any time soon. Having Craig in my home calls for such measures. In times of stress, I seek solace in increased levels of personal hygiene. I always shower at least once a day, without fail. If I'm anxious this can increase to two or three. Since Craig invaded my home, I've been having up to five a day. And I couldn't care less about the impact using so much water and energy might have on the environment. My priorities lie elsewhere. I am just finishing off another bottle of shower gel, when I hear the intercom. As I turn off the shower and jump out, I hear Craig walking towards the intercom.

"Craig," I shout whilst quickly dressing, "don't answer that." But it's too late. As I open the door, Craig is buzzing up whoever has rung, without even checking who it is.

"What the fuck are you doing?" I yell. "That could be anyone."

"Like who? Who ever visits you, you miserable cunt? It's probably a fucking Jehovah's Witness or something."

"Or someone looking for you maybe?"

"Oh shit, I never thought about that," he says, suddenly a little worried.

"Obviously not. Go and hide in the bedroom. And don't touch or wipe your dick on anything."

Craig runs and closes the bedroom door just as there is a knock at the front door. I open it slowly, and am deeply relieved to see Darren and Jimmy standing there.

"Oh it's just you two."

"Well who else were you expecting?" asks Jimmy.

"No one," I say, "I just wasn't expecting any visitors."

"We were just heading over to the pub," says Darren, "we haven't heard from you for a while, and we thought we'd see if you fancied a few pints."

"Thanks for the offer, but it's a bit awkward tonight, maybe I'll see you next—" I am stopped mid-sentence by a look of terror on both Darren and Jimmy's faces. They're looking over my shoulder towards the opposite end of the hallway. I turn around and am equally horrified to see that Craig has emerged from the bedroom.

"Well if it isn't left tit and right tit," he says.

"Oh god," Darren says, as though he's seen a ghost. "I didn't know... I mean. I thought you were in the army?"

"I was, but I've come back to spend some time with me old mate Gazza," Craig says, putting his arm around my shoulder. "How are you lads doing? I believe you're into cock these days eh Jimmy? How's that working out for you?"

"CRAIG!" I shout. Jimmy is lost for words, and looks at me accusingly. A lame shrug of the shoulders is the only apology I can offer. Craig turns his attention to Darren.   "And what about you? You're still with that Aimee bird I hear?"

"Bird?" Darren repeats incredulously. "Yes I'm still with her." He turns to me.   "Sorry Gaz we didn't realise you had company, we'll get off mate."

"No don't do that," Craig says, jumping between them and the door, "I thought we were all going to the pub? That'll be great, give us all a chance to catch up, talk about old times, that sort of thing. Then we can all go to a club and find some Birko slags. Well, not you, obviously Jimmy. But you can watch me having a piss or something if that'll get you hard."

"No way," I interrupt, "we're staying in tonight."

I usher Jimmy and Darren out of the door and onto the staircase.

"See you both soon," Craig can be heard saying as I pull the door closed.

"What the fuck is that psycho doing here?" They ask simultaneously.

"I assumed he was dead," Says Darren.

"Why would you assume that?" I ask.

"Well it's been so long since you mentioned him or anything. And he's just kind of the type to get himself killed in some stupid fight in a pub or something."

"Well as you can see," I say "he's very much alive. It's a bit complicated, but he's just staying with me for the time being."

"The place is a fucking mess, it looks like the devil lives there, and you look like crap," Jimmy points out correctly, "are you OK? What's been going on?"

I remember that they are both still unaware of what I did to Richard, but can't imagine how to even begin explaining it all to them.

"I'm fine. Well, I'm not fine, clearly I'm not fine, but its OK, it'll only be for a while. I hope. I'm sorry, I don't mean to shoo you out like this, but I think it's best if you don't call round while he's here."

"Don't worry, we wont," Darren says. "Just give us a call when he's gone."

Darren and Jimmy leave and I go back into the flat, where Craig is now stretched out on the couch, a rollie in his mouth and a can of lager in his hand. For some reason he has also taken his trousers off, but still has his shoes on. He turns to look at me.

"Well they were a tad frosty weren't they?" he asks.

"What? Are you taking the piss?"

"No, I thought they were decidedly unfriendly. I was being my usual outgoing self, and it almost seemed like they weren't pleased to see me."

"Of course they weren't pleased to see you. Who would be pleased to see you when you come out with the kind of shit you did just then."

"What shit?" he asks.

"That shit about Jimmy liking cock! Why the fuck did you have to say that? I told you not to say anything about that if you saw him. And referring to Aimee as a 'bird'. What the fuck were you thinking?"

"Oh that," he says, unimpressed, "I was only messing. Christ, if Jimmy can't take a bit of a joke about liking cock, then he shouldn't have decided to be gay in the first place should he? And what's so bad about calling Aimee a bird? It's not like I called her his bitch, or his ho' or anything like that."

"I know but it's still offensive," I say.

"Oh fuck off Gaz; you know full well I can be far more offensive than that if I want to. And believe me, I would want to be to that pair of wankers."

"Don't call them wankers, they're my friends," I protest.

"Friends? You've got no fucking idea what a friend is lad. The only reason you consider Laurel and fucking Hardy there to be mates is that they fucking tip-toe around you and indulge you. A real friend would just tell you what a fucking weirdo you are, like I do. They're only friends with you because you make them feel better about themselves."

"What's that supposed to mean?" I ask. Craig stands up and steps towards me, dropping his rollie into his can as he does so.

"I'll tell you what it means. That Darren is one of the most boring fuckers on the planet. Jesus, he married his childhood girlfriend. I mean, who the fuck is so sad that they would actually do that these days? He likes being friends with you because you make him feel better about himself. He probably thinks, 'well I may be a sad, boring twat, but at least I'm not a desperate and lonely freak like Gary'. And as for Rear Admiral Jimmy, well you make even his warped inclinations seem normal."

"He is normal," I say with a lack conviction that even I notice.

"Oh right yeah," Craig says, laughing openly, "you almost sound as though you actually believe that. I mean, there's nothing more normal than having another bloke's semen up your anus is there Gaz? Face it, your... association with those bell-ends isn't anything like friendship. You just use each other to make yourselves feel better. You use them because they let you get away with being such a fucking hopeless case, and they use you to make their own sad fucking lives seem a little bit better."

I'm stunned by this impromptu tirade, and I'm ready for a tirade of my own.

"Who the fuck do you think you are to judge people like that? Fucking hell, you're in another man's home, basically on the run from the army because you ripped some poor bastard's fucking nose off! Since when does someone who calls themselves 'Buckle' have the right to criticise other people's life choices? You haven't even got any fucking trousers on! You're a fucking lunatic, all you do is cause chaos. Since you came back you've been nothing but fucking trouble for me. Why don't you just fuck off out of my life and leave me alone?"

"Fine with me you cunt," he says, "I was getting fucking sick of it here anyway."

He grabs the small bag of belongings he brought with him, picks up his trousers and heads through the door without actually putting them on.

"Good fucking riddance you sociopath," I shout as he slams the door.

I take a few deep breaths and wait for my heart rate to settle. I sit down on the couch that has been taken over for the last couple of weeks and survey the bomb site that used to be my lounge.

"Fucking hell," I say aloud. I grab my coat and run through the door, down the stairs and out onto the street. I look down my road and can just about make out Craig as he turns the corner, still carrying his trousers in his hand. I run after him and catch him up about fifty yards along Balls Road.

"Craig, wait," I shout after him.

"Fuck off," he shouts back without either slowing down or turning his head.

"Where are you gonna go now?" I ask.

"Don't act as though you give a fuck," he says, finally turning his head slightly to acknowledge me.

"Come on," I say, "come back to the flat, you haven't got anywhere else to go. You still haven't even got any trousers on."

Craig stops and turns to face me.

"Why do you want me to come back?"

"I don't know," I say, "I just don't like the idea of you heading off with nowhere to go."

"Oh really? Is that all it is?"

"What do you mean?"

"I mean did I actually get through to you maybe? Did I open your fucking eyes, even just for a second? Did a little bit of what I said manage to penetrate the defences in that oh-so-fucking-complex brain of yours?"

"No, that's not it, it's just that you haven't got anywhere else to go."

"Fucking bollocks. Admit it, after all these years of your fucking solitude, of giving in to all the hate and anger you feel, after years of therapy and medication and fuck knows what else,

173

none of which had improved you in the fucking slightest, was all it took just a few home truths from a friend? Was that all it took to open your eyes at long fucking last?"

I look away from Craig, lost for words. I notice a police car coming along Balls Road towards us.

"Shit, there's a police car behind you," I whisper.

"I don't give a fuck," he says, not lowering his voice even a little. The police car pulls up alongside us.

"Fucking hell Craig, they've stopped, what are we gonna do?" I ask, panicking.

"Oh stop worrying you tit, they're probably just going the chippy."

As he speaks, two police officers get out of the car. The driver stands by his door, while the passenger approaches us.

"Is everything OK here lads?" he asks.

"Chippy's over there mate," Craig says, nodding his head in the direction of the chip shop.

"I beg your pardon?" asks the officer.

"Everything's fine, thanks," I say. He looks at me suspiciously, then turns back to Craig.

"Can I ask why you're not wearing any trousers?"

"You can ask I suppose," Craig says without looking at him.

"Why aren't you wearing any trousers?"

"No reason."

"Well I'm afraid I'm going to have to ask you to put them on, you can't be wondering around the streets with no trousers on, people might—"

"Yeah, yeah" Craig interrupts, "I'll put them on in a minute."

"Sir, I'm going to have to ask you to put them on now."

"Listen, *Cunt*stable, I'm trying to have a private fucking conversation here."

"Sir," he says, his tone changing from friendly to firm, "there's no need for that kind of language."

"Oh but I'd say there was every fucking need for it, Serpico," says Craig, apparently as impatient and annoyed as the officer, "I've told you I'll put me keks on in a minute, but right now I'm trying to talk to a friend. Now I can't do anything about all the fucking miscarriages of justice, all the racial persecution and fuck knows what else carried out by you and your fucking

174

cronies over the years, but I'll be *fucked* if I'm about to let you, on top of all that other shit, interrupt my private conversation. So why don't you and your boyfriend over there just get back in your car and fuck off?"

"Craig!!" I say, clearly far more aware of the growing severity of the situation than he is, then turn to the copper. "I'm sorry officer, he didn't mean that, he's just a bit upset. He's had a tragedy in his family recently and it's affecting him a bit. I'm gonna take him home now, and I'll make sure he stays out of trouble."

I realise my choice of words, and Craig's partial state of undress, probably make this seem like a domestic dispute, but I decide this is preferable to Craig getting himself arrested, but my words of placation appear to have been ineffective.

"I'll need to take your names," he says, producing a notepad from his pocket. He looks back to me. "Name?"

"Gary Lennon."

"And what's your address please Mr Lennon?"

"Flat four, number thirteen, James Street." My voice quivers slightly as I answer, and I can't take my eyes off Craig, who has been staring at the ground during this exchange. The copper turns towards him.

"And your name please?" Craig doesn't answer. "Your name please, *sir.*"

"Craig," I urge, "just answer him."

Craig sighs impatiently, and turns to face the officer of the law.

"The name's 'Buckle', fuck face." And without warning, he swats the officer's hat from his head with the back of his hand. Before either police can react, Craig drops his bag and his trousers onto the floor and stands with both arms held aloft, and yells at the top of his lungs:

"BUCKLE!!!!!!!!"

Finally the police spring into action. The first officer attempts to rugby tackle Craig, who deftly sidesteps him, kicking him up the arse as he flies past him and falls crashing to the ground. The second grabs Craig from behind, only to receive an elbow to the ribs, and a backwards head butt to the face. I find myself frozen to the spot, caught between a desire to aid my friend, and a desire not to be arrested. Craig must sense my indecision.

"Don't get involved Gaz," he says, holding his hand up to me. He sees the first policeman attempting to get back to his feet, and takes a small run up towards him, then administers a perfectly aimed kick right to the coppers arsehole.

"AAAAARRRRRGGHHHH!" he yells in pain as the tip of Craig's shoe briefly disappears between his buttocks.

"That's for Ian Tomlinson you fucking bastard cunt!" Craig shouts at him.

With his attention focused on his felled foe, Craig fails to notice that the second officer has regained his composure. He grabs Craig from behind, this time pulling Craig's arms behind him. By now the other officer has recovered sufficiently from his kick to the arse and is able to assist his colleague as he uses his radio to call for back up. They pin Craig face down on the ground so he can barely move. This doesn't stop him trying though, and he proceeds to make things as difficult for his captors as he possibly can, writhing around, spitting, thrashing his head and kicking his legs.

"BUCKLE!!! BUCKLE!!! BUCKLE!!!" he shouts, to the obvious bemusement of the police. Even when they deploy their pepper spray into his face, he doesn't stop thrashing, kicking and screaming during the few minutes it takes for a police van to arrive, at which point it requires five burly coppers to bundle him into the back of it.

"Which station are you taking him to?" I ask the arresting officer.

"I think you'd better go home mate," he answers.

"I want to know which station you're taking him to first," I protest. He turns towards me and points his finger at my face.

"I said go home lad, unless you wanna get nicked too!"

"Now you listen to me," I say assertively, "that's my friend in there. To you he might just be another psycho who you have to throw into the back of a van before beating him up down at the station, but he's my friend. I haven't committed any crime. If you disagree with me, then feel free to arrest me, and throw me into the back of that van too, but I am not going anywhere until I know where my friend is being taken."

"Grange Road station," he says, and gets into his police car and drives away. I look down at the floor and see Craig's trousers and bag.

"He hasn't even got any trousers on," I yell after the police vehicles as they speed away.

I run flat out for twenty solid minutes, with what Craig said to me back at my flat echoing around inside my brain, until I reach the police station where he is being held. I walk into the reception to see that the place seems completely empty other than me and the one policeman behind the front desk. He sits writing notes of some kind as I approach him.

"Can I help you sir?" he asks without looking away from his work.

"Yes," I say in my most polite voice, "I believe you're holding a friend of mine here."

"What's his name please?"

"Erm… well his name is Craig Macintyre, but he probably won't have told you that yet. But I think you'll know who I'm talking about by now anyway."

"Ah, so you're a friend of 'Buckle' then are you?" he asks, placing his pen down and suddenly giving me his undivided attention. "Well at least now we can put a real name in the register. And how exactly can I help you sir?"

"I was wondering if it'd be at all possible for me to see him for a few minutes please?"

"I'm afraid not sir, the only visitors we allow into the holding cells are solicitors. He'll be here for at least a good few hours, it's probably best if you go home, and wait for a phone call."

He turns his attention back to his notes. I turn and take a few steps towards the door, but stop before I get there. I wait in silence for a few seconds before walking back to the desk, and clear my throat loudly to attract his attention again.

"Yes sir, how can I help you?" he says facetiously.

"Yes, I would really appreciate it if you could let me see my friend for just a few moments. I know it's probably not the usual procedure, but the current situation my friend and I find ourselves in is a fairly unusual one. You see, just before his arrest, Craig was telling me some things. Some home truths that I think I've been needing to hear for a long time, and that nobody else has ever really been brave or honest enough to tell me, and if they have, well, I just haven't listened to them. And, for reasons that will soon become apparent to you and your colleagues, we will be prevented from resolving the conversation we were having. It is therefore very important to me that I am able to speak to him now."

The officer has been listening to me with a mixture of fascination and impatience.

"That's all very... informative. Clearly you and you friend were sharing something very deep and meaningful. Apparently what your friend had to tell you has had a profound effect upon you." I begin to smile, surprised that he has taken what I have had to say to heart. "But," he goes on, "I'm afraid it doesn't really change anything. I still really can't let you—"

"Look," I say, grabbing one of his wrists tightly in each of my hands and pulling him towards me, leaning in so our faces are just inches apart, "I understand that you are an officer of the law, and are sworn and duty-bound to uphold certain rules, regulations and procedures. But there are some things for which there can be no rules, no procedures, and the situation my friend and I find ourselves in qualifies as such a set of circumstances. What we were discussing is potentially life changing for at least one of us. Now I implore you, not as a police officer, but as a fellow human being, to forego those rules just once, and to please allow me to see my friend this one time."

He pulls his wrists from my grasp and fixes me with a steely gaze. I fear my impassioned plea has fallen on deaf ears, and I am more likely to be thrown into a cell myself than allowed to see Craig.

"You've got two minutes," he says.

As the door of the cell is swung open for me, Craig is sat on the bench, his legs crossed, looking down at his feet.

"I thought I told you fucking pigs to fuck off and leave me alone," he says without looking up.

"Craig, it's me," I say as the door is slammed shut behind me.

"Fuck me Gaz," he says as he lifts his head up, revealing two eyes reddened and bloodshot from the pepper spray, "what is this, a daring rescue or something?" He glances down at my hand. "If it is I hope you've come armed with more than a pair of my fucking trousers."

"Oh right, here you go." I hand Craig his trousers and sit down next to him on the bench.

"So then," says the now fully dressed Craig, "to what do I owe this unexpected visit?"

"I don't know. I just felt like I had to see you and speak to you again before they... do whatever it is they're going to do to you. So what exactly does happen to someone in your situation?"

"Fuck knows mate," he says, casually shrugging his shoulders, "I mean it's not as though I've been AWOL before. I suppose I'll be handed over to the army first of all. Then I'll be court-martialled or whatever. Then maybe I'll be prosecuted for ripping that bloke's nose off, assuming they even know it was me that did it. Either way, it looks like it's all gone a bit fuck-shaped for your old mate Buckle."

"Shit," I say, "I'm really sorry mate."

"Fuck that mate, don't be sorry for me. Have I ever given you the impression I'm bothered what happens to me? I don't give a fuck what they do Gaz. Que sera fucking sera. They can bang me up or execute me or do whatever the fuck they want, I really don't care."

"I didn't just mean that I'm sorry about that. I meant that I'm sorry about what I said to you back at my flat. I shouldn't have said some of those things."

"Of course you fucking should," says Craig, suddenly becoming more animated, "most of what you said was true. I mean, I do cause chaos wherever I go. I always have done, but I don't care, it's just the way I live my life Gaz. I'm a fucking force of nature. I say what I think and I do what I want. I fight and I fuck, and I couldn't care less what the fucking consequences are, and if other people don't like it then they'd best just keep out of my way. And if my actions end me up in jail, or court-martialled or even fucking dead, then that's fine with me. For twenty-nine years, Gaz, I've lived my life exactly the fucking way I want, and I've enjoyed every fucking minute of it. Well, most of it anyway. Can I ask you a question?"

"Go on then," I say apprehensively.

"How much of *your* life have you actually enjoyed?"

I am stunned that, for the second time in as many weeks, I burst into tears.

"Not very much of it," I admit through the sobbing.

"Exactly mate. That's the difference between us. You might think I'm a complete fucking psycho, and you're probably right. But I enjoy my life Gaz, and you waste half of yours cleaning your flat, switching your lights on and off a certain number of times, rearranging your fucking socks or whatever the fuck it is people like you do."

"I can't help the way I am though Craig," I say, wiping tears away from my face, "just as you didn't choose to be a psycho; I didn't choose to be as much of a fuck up as I am. I know nothing made me like this, I know it's nobody's fault, but I still can't help it. Do you think I actually *want* to waste my time doing things like that?"

"I don't fucking know what you do or don't wanna do. I'm not a fucking shrink am I? All I know is that you can choose to indulge all your little fucking compulsions and routines or whatever it is you call them if you want, but you know deep down that you're just using those things as an excuse not to lead a real life. And if you're not gonna choose to lead a life that is in some way worth living, then what's the fucking point of living at all? You'd might as well just fucking kill yourself. And we both know you're too much of a fanny to ever do that, so you might as well make some sort of attempt to enjoy life." He puts his arm around my shoulder and pulls me close to him. "You've wasted the first twenty-nine years of your life Gaz, for fuck's sake, please don't waste the rest of it."

Just then the door of the cell re-opens, and the copper steps in.

"Come on, your time's up mate," he says.

"What is it with you cunts?" Craig shouts at the startle officer. "Is it impossible to have a private conversation without one of you fuckers interrupting it?"

"It's alright Craig," I say before another situation develops, "he said he'd give me two minutes, and I think we've had a bit more than that. It's time for me to go."

We both stand up and I begin to walk towards the door, but Craig pulls me back and grabs me in a big, powerful bear hug. At first I stand rigid, not sure how to respond. 'Just fucking hug the mad bastard," I think to myself, and I wrap my arms around Craig's waist and hug him as hard as I possibly can.

"Remember what I said," he whispers into my ear, "don't waste anymore of your fucking life."

Craig kisses me on the cheek, and again I feel the tears streaming down my face.

"Goodbye Craig," I say, and I run out of the cell, past the copper, and out into the street, where the rain is hammering down and a strong wind is blowing. I look up at the grey Birkenhead sky, with its black clouds, its rain that burns the skin and stings the eyes. I have always loathed these skies, this rain, but now, I walk into the middle of the road, drop to my knees, hold open my arms, and embrace them. Cars swerve around me as I feel the rain cleansing me of my old ways, the swirling wind blowing an old way of life out of me, and in its place is a determination not to live the rest of my life in the shadows, and a realisation that maybe, just maybe, the world is not a cold dead place. In the rain-filled gutters of Birkenhead, I'm reborn.

I reach into my pocket and find a crumpled piece of paper, and instantly think of one way I can follow Craig's advice and begin to live a life that is actually worth living. I run to the phone box around the corner and step inside. I reach towards the receiver but pause momentarily before I can pick it up, and think of how many people have touched this phone, of people rubbing dog shit onto payphone receivers. I consider searching in my pocket for a hand-wipe.

"Fuck it," I say aloud, and pick up the receiver with my bare hand. With a trembling finger I dial the number on the piece of paper. After a few rings, the phone is picked up at the other end.

"Hello?"

I take a deep breath before I speak.

"Jenny, it's me, Gary. I... I want... I want to see you..."

And I wait for my life to begin.

Available from Armley Press

Coming Out as a Bowie Fan in Leeds, Yorkshire, England
By Mick McCann
ISBN 0-9554699-0-2

Hot Knife
By John Lake
ISBN 0-9554699-1-0

Nailed – Digital Stalking in Leeds, Yorkshire, England
By Mick McCann
ISBN 0-955469-2-9

How Leeds Changed the World – Encyclopaedia Leeds
By Mick McCann
ISBN 0-955469-3-0

Blowback
By John Lake
ISBN 0-9554699-4-7

Speedbomb
By John Lake
ISBN 0-9554699-5-4

In All Beginnings
By Ray Brown
ISBN 0-9554699-6-1

Leeds, The Biography: A History of Leeds in Short Stories
By Chris Nickson
ISBN 0-9554699-7-X

Reliability of Rope
By Samantha Priestley
ISBN 0-9554699-8-8

CPSIA information can be obtained at www.ICGtesting.com
Printed in the USA
LVOW07s1313081115

461583LV00005B/149/P